MARTY

Conflicts on the Campus

MARTY

Conflicts on the Campus

Nancy Wiley

MOODY PRESS

CHICAGO

To my mother

Printed in the United States of America

Contents

1

Coastal Bible College

THE BUILDING SITE which overlooked the city lights from its hillside perch was deserted. As the little sports car climbed its way past other similarly deserted lots toward the one at the top, Marty Miller stared out the side window with an air of concentration.

"That's it," said Richie Campbell to his companion, "the one at the very top. Dad forked over a pile for—" He turned to Marty and saw that she wasn't even looking. Richie's mouth tightened, and he stepped down on the accelerator, making the little car bounce over the rocks and rough patches in the unpaved road. He pulled into the lot and guided the car to the farthest edge, where he stepped on the emergency and turned off the ignition. With a disgusted huff he sat back, tapping his fingers on the steering wheel.

Marty turned to him apologetically, "I'm sorry, Rich."

"Fantastic view of the city, our own private lovin' patch, and you couldn't care less," he muttered, still drumming his fingers on the wheel.

"Come off it," she pleaded. "You're not making tonight any easier for me."

"Well, what do you want me to do?" he said, scowling. "Pat you on the head and agree that it's a rotten, lousy break that you're being shipped off to a convent instead of going to State with the rest of us? Would that really help, Marty?"

She made no reply, and Richie opened the door, eased himself out, and stretched. He reached back for her hand and pulled her across the front seat. "Let's walk a little," he said more compassionately. They sauntered along the stake-and-string fence erected by the workmen to denote a dangerous falloff on the property line. Richie put his arm around her as they walked, squeezing her against him several times. Her expression remained the same, without any reaction.

"It's just no good tonight, huh?" he said finally as they completed their circle of the property and approached the car.

She leaned against the fender. "I guess not."

Richie touched his lips to her forehead. "I'd like it to be. I'd like to have something special to remember you by over these next months." He kissed her softly again.

"You're not going to remember anyway," she replied with a touch of bitterness and pulled away from him. "Somehow I can't quite see Richie Campbell, God's gift to women, shutting himself up in some fraternity house writing letters to his high school sweetheart. Not while everybody else is partying around."

"Marty, I told you—"

"Don't make promises you can't keep." The tears began to trickle down her cheeks.

He shrugged his shoulders in a helpless gesture. "Do you want to go home now?"

"We might as well."

The young couple got back in the car and drove in silence down the winding road. At the stop sign by the highway Richie looked to Marty hopefully, but she shook her head. He turned right in the direction of the main streets of Santa Alberta. They passed the new shopping center still under construction, the plate-glass facade of their recent alma mater, Hoover High, and other familiar landmarks of this prosperous northern California suburb. Richie punched on the radio and made a left at the service station. He pulled up in front of the Miller home, a sloping bungalow.

"Mama left the porch light on for you." He grinned, trying to lighten her mood.

"Mama has become most careful these days," she replied, and the bitterness was no longer concealed.

"Is this it then? Good-bye?" Richie asked, sliding over to where he could put his arm around her.

"It has to be," said Marty with resignation.

"I do love you, doll, in spite of what you think," he assured, flashing a most appealing smile.

"Good night, Richie," she said, getting out.

"Hey— I can at least walk you to the door!"

She shook her head, not trusting her voice, and walked away from the proud little sports car and everything that had mattered for the past year and a half. She looked at her watch while digging through her purse for the house key. 11:30. That ought to please her folks for a change. Marty pushed the door open and entered the front hall. She could see into the living room where her mother was lying on the sofa with a magazine.

"Is that you, Marty?"

Who else would it be? she thought with disgust. But she answered an obedient, "Yes," and started for her room.

"Did you have a nice time, dear?" Her mother sat up and looked around.

The anger Marty had stifled all evening rose to the top and overflowed. She stalked back to the living room entrance and glowered. "No, Mother," she said coldly, struggling to maintain control. "I had a miserable time—just like I'm going to have from now on—thanks to you!" Overcome by tears, Marty ran down the hall and slammed the door to her room.

Joe Miller flicked off the TV in the family room and came to his wife's side. "She's taking it pretty hard, isn't she?" he observed.

Shirley looked at the still lean figure of the man she had married twenty-five years earlier and smiled. "Someday she'll understand, I hope. We've just got to trust the Lord that it's not too late."

Joe ran his hand over his balding head, then reached to adjust the thermostat for the night. "We're trying anyway, Shirl. You can't do anymore than that. I'm going to turn in."

His wife snapped off the reading lamp and laid her magazine on the coffee table. "If we'd tried this hard with Joyce—" she began, then let her voice trail off as she thought better of it.

"Is Joyce coming over to say good-bye in the morning?" he questioned.

"She and Danny will be here in time for breakfast."

"Al's working early tomorrow?"

"She didn't say," answered Shirley, catching up with him. She stopped in front of Marty's door and was satisfied that there were no audible sobs. "Good-night, Marty. I'll call you about six." There was no response.

*   *   *

Six o'clock and her mother's voice came abruptly to a weary Martha Miller. She slid her feet over the side of the bed and searched for a strayed slipper. Marty sighed and felt the rollers in her hair. She had considered not rolling it last night—there didn't seem to be much point—but pride had won out. The suitcases stood in front of the closet; the garment bag hung from a hook on the back of the door. September 17th was here at last. A squeal echoed from the hallway, and Marty knew that her little nephew had arrived. Unable to face Danny at this early hour, she decided to get dressed before breakfast. A skirt and blouse had been set aside; Mother had vetoed the idea of cutoffs even if they were more comfortable for traveling. She slipped into her clothes and sat down in front of the mirror to work on her hair. The reflected image was noted appreciatively—a heart-shaped face set off by loosely waved hair of a deep brown tone. With the touch of mascara which she now added, her green eyes sparkled. *Not bad,* she thought, standing up for a full-length view. *Shame to waste it on a bunch of would-be missionaries!* Marty smiled at this display of inflated ego.

"Martha!" called her mother from the kitchen. "Breakfast."

Marty abandoned the solace of her own room and joined the family at the table. Her sister, Joyce, was strapping eighteen-month-old Danny into the high chair.

"What brings you out so early?" said Marty, taking a seat.

"Couldn't let little sis leave for college without wishing her luck," answered Joyce, slumping into a chair. "Besides this isn't early for Danny. He's been up for an hour already!"

"Marriage and family getting you down?" teased Marty, drinking her juice.

"Martha," her father interrupted, "we haven't asked the blessing yet."

"Sorry, sorry, I sometimes forget about all our new habits," she commented cynically.

Her father ignored this and bowed his head. "Our Father, we thank Thee for this new day, and pray Thy blessing upon it and especially upon Marty as she begins school. We would ask for Thy protection as we travel. Bless this food now, for we ask it in Jesus' name. Amen."

Marty poured another glass of juice and looked across the table at her sister, who had deposited a handful of cold cereal on the baby's tray. Joyce didn't look like Joyce anymore—marriage had aged her five years. Sure it had been rough, but anyone who got messed up like that didn't deserve to have it easy. Watching Joyce pacify Danny's impatience, Marty thought back to that morning almost two years ago when the family had let her in on the big secret. Joyce and Al Stoddard were going to Yuma that day to be married.

"And there's no need to count on your fingers," Joyce had said belligerently. "The baby's due in March."

It had hurt at the time. Joyce and Marty, only a year apart in age and looking enough alike to be twins, had been closer than most sisters. Marty had never quite matched Joyce's record in school, but she had come close and had been flattered rather than resentful by the comparisons. But for all her brains, Joyce had been dumb. And now she was stuck with that slob, Al Stoddard. Marty had cried that night, but she had gotten over it quickly. Unfortunately her parents had not been able to brush it off and keep going. They had blamed themselves and blamed each other, and things were pretty hot for a while.

"You want another piece of toast?" her mother asked, breaking into these thoughts.

"No, thank you," replied Marty, getting up. "I've got to put a few things in my overnight case."

"If you'll watch your grandson," Joyce said to her mother, "maybe I can help." Pushing away from the table, she followed Marty into her room.

Marty gathered up several bottles and jars from the dresser top. She supposed that Joyce had come in to give her some "big sisterly" advice, which she could do without.

"You taking your bear?" asked Joyce, picking up the giant panda on the bed.

Marty glanced over at what had been for months her most treasured possession. Richie had won it for her at a carnival on their first date. "No," she replied flatly. "It's going to be hard enough to forget everything as it is." She stuck a scarf in the top of the case and closed the lid.

"Marty," Joyce began hesitantly, "I wish you'd look at this differently. Believe me, you've got a chance to find something really great in life. You don't have to make the same mistakes I did."

"Listen, Joyce." Marty turned angrily on her sister. "I have no intention of making your mistakes. You had your chance, and you blew it. If 'getting religion' now has helped you and the folks—if you get some sort of satisfaction out of walking aisles and blubbering in preachers' handkerchiefs—fine. That's your business. But why does everyone have to stuff it down my throat? Why am I being packed off to some fruity Bible school? I wasn't the one who got in trouble!"

Joyce was stung by these words, but Marty no longer cared.

"As a favor to someone who's sadder but wiser, will you give it a fair try?"

"I tell you what I'm going to do, and you can tell Mom and Dad if you want to. I'm going to find a job and save up enough money to transfer to State on my own. I'll sign Dad's name to the application papers if I have to, but I'm not going to stay at Coastal one minute longer than necessary."

"You about ready?" Mr. Miller called.

"You coming out to the car?" asked Marty, picking up a suitcase.

"Sure," her sister answered quietly. "I'll help you carry some of these."

Joe Miller opened the bedroom door and picked up the remaining pieces of luggage, and the procession, not unlike a group of mourners, filed slowly toward the front door.

* * *

The sun beat down on the Miller station wagon as it moved through the morning traffic. Marty, settled in the back with the baggage, gazed stoically out the window.

"How much farther is it?" Mr. Miller asked his wife, indicating with his head the map that lay on the dashboard.

She unfolded the bulky paper and traced their course with her finger. "Was that Hillsboro that we just came through?"

"Uh-huh." He nodded.

"Then we're about twenty-five miles from Harwood."

"Good." He smiled. "We ought to make it by nine o'clock easy. Registration's from nine to eleven, isn't it, Marty?"

The effort to draw his daughter into the conversation failed as she muttered, "I think so," and continued to stare at the passing scenery. It was getting warmer with each mile of the trip. Marty thought maliciously, *Someone ought to sue this school for false advertising. "Coastal" Bible College—ha! It might be on the Western coast of the North American continent, but the San Joachin Valley is certainly not a seaside resort.* Through-out most of the drive she had managed to shut off reality and enjoy a delightful fantasy of how Richie would be fighting off the captain of the State football team for the privilege of dating her after she transferred. Now, with only twenty-five miles be-tween herself and virtual imprisonment, she considered for the first time what it might be like. She had seen the catalog and knew what courses she wanted. It seemed possible that some of them might be accepted at State. Marty shifted her position and gazed at the backs of her parents' heads. *They could be worse,* she admitted. *They think they're doing right, and they're suffer-ing about as much as I am. And they ought to,* she reasoned, not willing to be carried away with sympathy for them. But bowing to sentiment, she resolved to be civil to her parents for the remainder of the trip.

"When are you going to come home for a visit?" Mr. Miller asked, trying again.

"The first chance I get, Dad," Marty answered positively. "The first chance I get."

Embarrassed smiles of relief swept across both of the parental faces, and her mother turned around and patted her arm.

* * *

Jeanne Robbins arrived in Harwood that morning about the same time Marty was waking up, and she had expected the bus terminal to be somewhat larger. To be sure, it was an improve-ment over the desert stops of the preceding night, but there was a depressing similarity in the dingy walls and dim lighting. She followed two other passengers over to the baggage stand and presented her claim tickets. Three large suitcases and one se-curely bound cardboard box were too much for an eighteen-year-old girl to manage alone, but there were no offers of help. Jeanne moved them one at a time to a nearby bench and sat down to wait. The group around the baggage stand was break-ing up, and she watched them file out the main door into the darkness, all apparently sure of a destination. The large wall clock showed plainly that it was only quarter to six—much too early to put in a call to the school. Looking around, she realized that even the terminal employee who had checked her luggage had now disappeared. The barnlike waiting room was deserted.

She put the sweater she had been carrying over her shoulders. September in central California is usually warm even in the early morning hours, but Jeanne felt chilled, and tired as well. The bus trip had been too big an event for sleeping across those desolate desert stretches. She picked up her purse to check again whether the paper with the phone number was still tucked in the side pocket. It was, of course, and the dime she had been saving was there with it. She gazed about the room, located a phone booth, and then leaned back against the hard frame—to wait.

"So I said to him, 'What more can you expect?' "

"Right, right."

Jeanne sat up and turned toward the sound of the voices. Two sailors emerged from the men's room and were walking in her direction. They stopped at the newsstand to look over last night's headlines. Jeanne's stomach felt like lead, but she managed to resume breathing. Her eyes darted across the room for a possible escape route. She was closer to the main door than the sailors were.

"You're sure you won't change your mind?" the taller of the navy men addressed his companion.

"No, it'd just be a lot of trouble, but thanks anyway, Harry," the other replied.

"OK, then, we'll see you in a day or so." Sailor number one, with duffel bag over his shoulder, headed for the main door. Jeanne felt he was eyeing her as he walked, but she couldn't be certain without looking up; and she didn't want them to think she was interested.

The front door swung shut behind the departing seaman, and from the corner of her eye Jeanne observed that the other man had turned back to the newsstand. A coin clinked loudly in the vending machine as he made his selection. Jeanne risked taking a good look at him, reminding herself that she might need to be able to give a description later, and was surprised to discover that he was young and attractive. She turned her head quickly as he picked up his bag and started toward her. Staring steadily at the contents of her purse, she listened to his approaching footsteps. The bench swayed slightly as he took a seat on the opposite end. Ten feet away—and it was only twelve minutes to six.

Jeanne prayed as she never had before, "Dear God, don't let anything happen! Guide me, protect me, show me what to do." It came to mind that if she hummed a familiar hymn, the sailor would at least know what kind of girl she was. Hesitatingly she began with a few bars of "The Old Rugged Cross," but the sound of her own voice in that vast, empty waiting room was all the more terrifying. She stole a glance at the other end of the bench; the sailor was reading his paper. If she could only hold him off for a while.

At six o'clock an older couple entered the terminal. Minutes later the lights popped on inside the enclosed snack bar, and a white-shirted man began preparations for breakfast. It had worked. The sailor was still reading, and Jeanne dared to relax a little. Across the way two bus company employees emerged from a door marked "No Admittance." One unlocked the ticket office; the other posted a new arrival time for the bus from Los Angeles. More people arrived by way of the main door, and a bustle of activity had now replaced the haunted silence of a few minutes earlier.

The sailor laid his paper aside, collected his various belongings, and stood up. He stretched and, throwing his bag over his shoulder, sauntered off in the direction of the snack area.

For the moment Jeanne was overwhelmed with relief. She smiled to herself, but her gratitude for deliverance could not entirely crowd out a minute tug of disappointment. Not even a sailor was interested in her.

*   *   *

Paul Herbert eased his wiry frame out of the car and stood quietly breathing the freshness of the September morning. The penetrating warmth of the valley sun was a burden to most of its inhabitants, but Herbert found it comfortable and invigorating. The parking lot was almost half full, and he looked vainly for a familiar face among those unloading suitcases and possessions. He saw none, but this was to be expected since the day had been reserved for the registration of incoming freshmen. The sloping pathway that led from the lot to the main campus seemed more of an obstacle to his seventy-one years than he had remembered it from last June. With determination he joined the families and students who were following the hand-lettered signs toward the main door of Harrison Hall.

"Morning, Doc!" called a broad-shouldered young man as Herbert passed his car.

"Good morning," he replied with a smile, trying desperately to connect the face with a name from some grade book of the past. The connection wasn't there, so he hastened his step to avoid further conversation. The landscaping of Coastal Bible College had undergone some renovations during the summer months, and Dr. Herbert viewed the trimmed hedges and patches of flowers appreciatively. The pain in his knee and the ache in his back reminded him that his task was not sightseeing but simply conquering that stubbornly inclined path. He was encouraged when a parting of the oak trees revealed the rambling Mediterranean-styled edifice that housed the school's classrooms, offices, library and dining area. Harrison Hall's available space was greatly overtaxed, but to Dr. Herbert the inconveniences, accepted cheerfully by faculty and students alike, were a part of the incontestable charm of the school.

Reaching level ground, the professor was pleased to see the

campus busy with activity. The situation at Coastal had changed noticeably over the past five years. He smiled to himself thinking of those days, not so long past, when the members of the faculty and staff had been on their knees trusting God for a few students. Now the prayer meetings centered upon requests for buildings to hold the abundance of applicants the Lord had so faithfully provided. Paul Herbert was filled with gratitude for having been a part of this movement.

Two long tables had been borrowed from the library and placed on either side of Harrison Hall's main door. Miss Griswold, the registrar, and her crew of student assistants were handing out the housing assignments and answering the multitude of questions.

"Good morning, Dr. Herbert," was Miss Griswold's crisp greeting as he approached the table. "I thought perhaps you might desert us this year for some more interesting pastime."

"No, Miss Griswold, I'm a little older and slower, but I wouldn't miss the opportunity of taking an early peek at this year's crop."

"Can I find you a chair?"

"No, thank you," he replied, sitting down carefully on the top step of Harrison's entrance. "I'm able to see everything very well from here."

Miss Griswold adjusted her glasses and returned to her work. Waiting for her attention was a well-dressed family group, and Dr. Herbert concentrated on his favorite game of amateur analysis. The parents in this case appeared to be financially comfortable, but the lines in their faces as well as their expressions imparted a history of personal difficulties. A recent tragedy, perhaps, guessed the professor, or just the trials of a teenaged daughter in the home? The daughter in question hung back from her parents and seemed shy or reluctant to get on with the process of initial registration. She was an attractive girl with fine features, and Dr. Herbert noticed with admiration her loose-flowing dark hair. He was glad to see this trend toward longer hair; it reminded him of the way Frieda had worn hers when they first met. The accompanying trend to shorter and tighter skirts for the young ladies was not so much to his taste. *Perhaps I'm getting too old to appreciate that,* he mused.

"Welcome to Coastal," Miss Griswold greeted the couple and peeked around them for a glimpse of the girl.

"Thank you," the man responded. "I'm Joe Miller from Santa Alberta. This is my wife, Shirley," he said, nodding to the woman at his side, "and our daughter, Martha." He turned and motioned to the girl to come closer. She moved silently to the table and stood expressionless facing Miss Griswold.

"Yes, yes, of course." The registrar nodded her head mechanically, as was her habit, at the same time searching through the stack of cards spread before her. "Ah, yes, here it is." She looked up at the dark-haired girl and commented, "It will be a pleasure having you with us, Martha. You will be located in Room 108, that's on the second floor of the women's dorm, and your roommate will be Jeanne Robbins from Arizona. I don't think she has checked in yet, but you may go over to your room and unpack your things." Miss Griswold hesitated, expecting some sort of response. When none came, she looked more closely into the girl's eyes and saw what she feared might be a spark of bitterness or contempt. Ignoring this purposely, she continued, "I trust that we can be of help to you this year, and that the Lord will make you a real blessing to all of us."

"I wouldn't count on it." Marty Miller stared coldly at the older woman and then walked away. Her mother appeared embarrassed and started to say something, but Mr. Miller took her by the arm, and they followed after their daughter.

"A real eager beaver," commented Barbara Sheldon who was seated next to Miss Griswold and occupied with stamping a set of forms.

Dr. Herbert started to make a mental note of the name, thought better of it, and drew a battered envelope from his inside coat pocket. His script was as uncertain as his memory, but this would serve as a prayer reminder, and he wrote her name down. A hand clasped his shoulder.

"You keeping track of the good-looking ones for me?" A lanky student with a good-natured grin sat down next to the professor.

"Peter!" Dr. Herbert exclaimed with a mingling of joy and surprise. "You did make it back! Well, praise the Lord. I've been praying all summer that God would open up some doors for you."

"Thanks, Doc," said Pete Bradley with sincerity. "I appreciate your interest. It's going to be living by faith this year, but I have enough for the first payment."

"A step at a time, boy. That's all He requires. What are you doing around here today?"

"Running errands for Dr. Todd, Miss Griswold, or anyone else who beckons," answered Pete, "and getting paid for it." His hair was sun-bleached, and the lean frame had been deeply browned during the summer months.

"You're looking exceptionally well," the professor appraised. "Have you been working outdoors? Lifeguard or something?"

The young fellow laughed. "Nothing so romantic or interesting, just spent the summer in the fields up home."

"Well—" Dr. Herbert began. But not having anything in particular to add to this observation, he allowed the word to dangle in air. Pete stood up, brushing off the seat of his pants.

"Say, if you're running errands for people, would you mind doing one for me?"

"Anytime."

Dr. Herbert handed him a four-by-six-inch card. "Would you post this on the main bulletin board?"

Pete took the card and disappeared through the arched doorway. He approached the reception desk and the bulletin board which stood next to it. A thumbtack secured the notice in the cork among many others, and Pete stepped back to read it.

"WANTED. Reliable girl to spend specific hours each week

as companion for older woman. Reasonable pay. Inquire of R. Paul Herbert, Chairman, Department of Modern Languages."

Pete shook his head with regret. Mrs. Herbert must be worse than before. Her antics had amused some, elicited pity from others for several years. But Doc had held his head high, and the sight of him watchfully escorting his beloved Frieda on their afternoon walk was familiar to the Harwood residents. Pete made his way back to the entrance, a little more slowly than before, trying to put himself in Dr. Herbert's position and finding it beyond the powers of his imagination. *A good man,* he thought, *I should do so well.*

"All taken care of," he announced to the professor, then walked over to Miss Griswold for further assignment. The phone, which had been extended to reach the outside table, rang.

"Would you catch that, Barbara?" requested Miss Griswold.

"Coastal Bible College, registrar's office— Yes, it is— Certainly, at the bus terminal— Yes, we'll send someone down right away— All right, good-bye." Barbara Sheldon looked up with a smile. "Freshmen!" she said with the superior air of an upperclassman. "There's one down at the bus terminal. She's been there since 6 A.M., but wasn't sure if she should call so early!"

The registrar glanced over at Pete. "Want the job?" Without waiting for an answer, she continued, "You can take the station wagon, and would you stop at the post office and mail these?"

Pete rejoiced at the opportunity of going to town, even if it meant coaxing a few more miles out of the old wagon. The car had been a well-intended gift from a friend of the school, but had 85,000 on the speedometer when it arrived. Its main function was running bus service over the four miles into Harwood. Earlier it had served the basketball team as transportation to out-of-town games, but now the players and coaches preferred to rely upon their own vehicles. Pete took the keys from Miss Griswold and ran easily down the path to the parking lot.

It was almost 9:30 when he pulled up in front of the terminal. There was no one waiting out in front, so he left the station wagon parked in a loading zone and went inside. Pete scanned the waiting room, hoping to pick out the prospective student. In his haste to be off before Miss Griswold changed her mind about sending him, he had forgotten to ask the girl's name. His eyes rested at last on a forlorn figure, seated on the end of a bench and surrounded by suitcases and boxes. Pete sighed and experienced a twinge of disappointment—another one to enhance the reputation of "Coastal Girls"—overweight, hair curled too tightly, clothes— He fortified himself for the task and ambled across the room.

"Are you the one who's waiting for a ride up to the college?" he inquired politely.

Jeanne jumped to her feet. "Yes, I am," she stammered, and reached down to gather up the luggage.

"I'll get those," Pete insisted. "The car's out in front." They left the terminal quickly, and Pete loaded Jeanne's belongings into the back of the wagon.

"Hop in," he directed, knowing that he should have gone around to open the door for her, but not caring too much. She hesitated as to whether he intended for her to get in front or in back, at last taking the chance that he meant for her to sit next to him.

"I've got to make a stop at the post office, and then we'll go right out to school," he said as the engine turned over successfully on the third try.

"Fine," responded Jeanne. She was undeniably excited and observed the stores with interest as they cruised down the main street of Harwood. "Are you a student at Coastal?" she asked, having summoned up sufficient courage to question her attractive companion.

Pete considered the possibility of telling her that he was Dr. Todd—she seemed innocent enough to believe it. However, he replied, "Yes. I'm Pete Bradley, a senior majoring in English and planning to go on to seminary next year."

Jeanne beamed her approval. "That's wonderful! I've waited so long to come to Coastal— I just can't believe I'm really here!"

Her enthusiasm and sincerity made Pete ashamed. He pulled over in front of the post office. "I hope the Lord makes it as wonderful for you as you've hoped." He smiled warmly. "This will just take a minute."

Jeanne watched him get out and bound up the front steps into the building. She had never met such a fine-looking Christian fellow before. Of course it was too much to even hope—but she was hoping just the same.

* * *

Marty sat on the edge of the bed and surveyed the disorder and confusion which she had brought to that tiny room. She wished that her folks hadn't been in such a hurry to leave, although she knew her dad was due back in the office that afternoon. Coastal Bible College had thus far fulfilled all of her expectations—dingy, crummy and square. Marty sighed. She didn't seem to have any tears left to shed, so she might as well start unpacking. The little alcove in the corner with the rod across it appeared to be the closet. She laughed, wondering how she would ever fit all of her clothes into that small space and whatever would her roommate do with her things.

A knock at the door startled Marty. "Come in," she answered hesitantly. The door opened to reveal an unusual-looking twosome. One girl was tall, broad-shouldered, her face a maze of freckles, and hair that resembled the remnants of a pillow fight. The other, in complete contrast, was petite and stylish.

"Wright and McMasters, your neighbors from across the hall," the tall girl boomed their introduction in a deep voice that was perfectly matched to the rest of her appearance.

In spite of her generally disagreeable mood, Marty was forced to smile back at the visitors. "I'm Marty Miller," she returned, "come on in."

The attractive little redhead spoke for the first time. "Don't mind Corrine's introduction. She's Wright; I'm Kathy McMasters." While she was speaking, Kathy inspected Marty's face as though she expected to find the key to an individual's personality in eye color or jaw structure. "How do you like it so far?" she continued with a disarming forwardness that caught Marty unprepared.

"Not very much," Marty answered honestly. "But then, I didn't expect to."

Kathy laughed. "That's just how I felt when I first came. Give yourself some time to appreciate it," she added gaily. "Can we help you unpack?"

"No thanks. Then you're not freshmen?" asked Marty, thinking afterward that it was probably a dumb question.

"High and mighty sophomores!" corrected Corrine who had been watching other new arrivals from the window. "Look!" she cried to her friend. "There's Pete!"

Kathy hurried over to see, and Marty joined them out of curiosity. The two older girls stood watching in silence. Marty looked over the students gathered on the lawn below without any certainty as to which one was the object of their interest.

"Who's Pete?" she asked finally.

"About the neatest guy on campus," Corrine answered with such evident feeling that her roommate patted her on the shoulder.

"Down, girl," Kathy cautioned. She turned to Marty, "Pete's the one by the station wagon. He's a confirmed woman hater, but that doesn't seem to bother Corrine."

Marty looked down at the lanky blond and decided that he didn't compare to Richie or a dozen guys she had known at home.

"Yikes!" squealed Corrine. "He's coming inside!" Bolting

for the door with prodigious leaps, she dived across the hall to the sanctuary of her own room.

Kathy shook her head. "That's my roommate!" she said. "If you decide you need some help later on, let us know." And she also disappeared into the hall, closing the door behind her. Marty sat down on the bed again, more puzzled than before. These girls didn't fit the image she had created for her fellow students at a Bible school, and she didn't feel like trying to figure out where they did fit in. The task of unpacking was still ahead.

Her thoughts were immediately interrupted by another knock. Before she could answer, the door opened, and there stood the prototype of what she had expected to find at Coastal. Behind her, loaded with suitcases and boxes, was Corrine's idol—the magnetic and mysterious Pete.

2

Joyce

JOYCE FOLDED the newspaper quietly and tiptoed out of the living room into the cubbyhole of a kitchen. She looked at her watch again, finding it hard to believe that it was already ten o'clock. Al would be home any minute and would want to know why the dishes weren't done yet. Joyce sighed as she began to run water in the sink. Her husband seemed to have no understanding of how much time could be spent placating a fussy baby, and Danny had really been going strong all day. She dumped a stack of plates into the suds and added silverware and glasses until there was no more room. At least it would look like she was working when Al came in. Her eye caught the calendar above the sink, and she reached up with a soapy hand to tear off September's sheet. In spite of the sudden crispness in the fall air, Joyce had failed to notice that another month was gone. Maybe it was because the days seemed to blend into one another without any variation in her routine or responsibilities.

The front door of the tiny apartment slammed. Grabbing a dish towel to dry her hands, Joyce hurried into the living room. Al dropped his shoes and a wet towel in the middle of the floor and sank into the overstuffed and out-of-shape chair.

"Danny's asleep," she cautioned.

"Good," he grunted in return.

The unnatural silence that had become a part of their mar-

26

riage in recent months hung over the small room. Joyce stood in the doorway, methodically wiping her hands; Al stared at the TV screen without expression. He was a large fellow without any distinguishing features. People meeting him for the first time were hard pressed afterward to describe his appearance, other than his "bigness."

"Wish we could get that thing fixed," he muttered, and instinctively Joyce felt that this was meant as criticism of her. "Got any beer?" he asked, looking her way for the first time.

"No." She shook her head.

"Didn't I tell you to get some this week?" His question was in the form of an accusation, and his cold gaze made her look away.

"I had to buy Danny's medicine out of the grocery money, remember?" She put the towel down and sat on the sofa. "There just wasn't enough left over for any extras this time."

"You didn't put anything in the collection plate at church last Sunday, I suppose?" A half smile played on his lips while awaiting her answer.

"Al, you promised—" she remonstrated. "Two dollars a week to spend any way I want to."

"So my beer money goes to feed a bunch of Africans."

Joyce held her tongue, aware that he was looking for an argument. She walked back to the sinkful of dishes, but her energy had been depleted and it seemed an effort just to remain on her feet. Al followed her into the kitchen and critically surveyed the disarray.

"How was the game?" she asked, hoping to channel his interests in another direction.

"There wasn't a game," he said, opening the refrigerator and taking out a carton of milk. "The league play doesn't start until the first part of December."

"Then why did you have to go tonight?"

"I went because I wanted to." He stopped pouring the milk and looked at her thoughtfully. "Do you ever listen to anything

I tell you about basketball or about anything that I happen to like?"

"Of course," she replied defensively.

"Then you ought to know that I need to get in shape early because I'll have to miss some of the practice games on the nights I work. Bailey's coaching this year, and he gives the guys he runs around with all the breaks anyway."

"Playing basketball really means a lot to you, doesn't it?"

"It's the only thing left that's any fun," he muttered sourly.

"But, Al, having 'fun' isn't all there is to life—" she began.

"Don't lecture me, Joyce. It's bad enough as it is." He finished the glass of milk and returned the carton to the refrigerator. Joyce watched him, unable to deny that she understood what he meant. She walked over to where he was standing and put her arms around his waist.

"I want it to be better, Al. I really do."

"Yeah, sure, baby. I know." He smiled, but the words had a weary and resigned tone.

"Couldn't I help you someway?" she asked hopefully. "You know, couldn't we invite the guys on the team over for an evening or something?"

A surprised expression crossed his face. "Would you really like to do that? You're always telling me what a bunch of crumbs those guys are."

"Maybe I just haven't had a chance to get to know them." In that moment Joyce had a glimmer of understanding about her marriage. It wasn't all Al's fault, and it wasn't just because they didn't have money. She recognized suddenly how set she had been that things be done her way, and she was ashamed.

"Let's see, today is Tuesday. Could we have them over Friday night? Would that give you enough time?" Al's voice was animated.

"Sure," she replied lightly, rejoicing in the idea of doing something together.

"Can the grocery budget afford it?"

She grinned. "For a special event, I think we could borrow a bit from next week."

He looked at her with a tenderness that had been absent for many months. "I love you, Joyce," he said softly.

"I'm glad," she replied. "I'm glad."

With his arm around her shoulder, he led her out of the kitchen, flipping off the light switch as they went. The dishes remained in the sink, unwashed and forgotten.

* * *

Paul Herbert had been at his desk for almost an hour when the sun finally rose above the flat range in the east. He gazed out the window, admiring as he did so the little patch of flowers that clung tenaciously to their summer bloom. He wondered vaguely if there would be time to plant a second bed next spring, and then caught himself wondering too much and not concentrating enough on the message he was preparing for chapel that morning. Again he wished he could remember whether or not he had used this text previously for a college gathering, although he realized with a rueful smile that no one would be apt to notice it if he had.

Unable to settle back to work, he rose slowly from his desk and walked into the kitchen. Hoping that coffee might help, he filled the new electric percolator with water and carefully measured out the coffee. Dr. Herbert was at home in the kitchen. For more years than he could remember he had been in charge of fixing meals as well as the general housekeeping. And in all honesty he was forced to admit that the little house had suffered under his care. Perhaps this girl who was staying with Frieda could help a little with the cleaning, he mused, knowing, however, that the elasticity of their budget had already reached its limitations. Coffee smells permeated the room, and the rich aroma transported him back to—he couldn't actually remember when, but sometime when life had been simple and uncomplicated. There always had been people in the kitchen in those days, sitting around the table with coffee cups and strips of

Frieda's *apfelkuchen* when he came in from afternoon classes. So often it had been Harold and his friends, solemnly thrashing over ideas, confident that they were on the edge of discovering answers to the questions that so confounded their elders. Harold. Had it really been twenty years since they had stood together in that crowded airport?

"I don't really mind so much, Dad. It isn't going to be forever." Those had been his words as he had boarded the plane. Dr. Herbert could see him clearly as he mounted the steps, a tan trench coat over his arm, an overnight bag in his hand— eager smile—blond crew cut. Had it really been twenty years! Peacetime operations—such a senseless waste—but within the perfect will and knowledge of a loving heavenly Father, he reminded himself, and was surprised to find his eyes moist and his lips trembling. The old man poured himself a cup of coffee and returned to his desk. He felt shaken, not so much for having relived again those last moments with his only son, for he had done that many times before. It was the realization that past and present became fused so often these days, and sometimes he found memory more comfortable than reality. He closed his books and put his head down on his arms, placing this burden upon a God who had never failed to provide daily grace in the times of need.

"I'll be there as soon as I locate my Bible," Frieda called from the bedroom. Dr. Herbert sat up suddenly. "Hurry, Harold, we don't want to be late this morning," she continued, and the house vibrated with the opening and shutting of dresser drawers. "I surely didn't leave it in here, did I?" Frieda Herbert appeared in the doorway dressed for church. Her good black coat, now several sizes too big, was fully buttoned, and a small flowered hat perched at a gay angle on her whitened hair. Since the burdens of worry and responsibility had been lifted, her face had assumed an air of peace; the wrinkles and creases had all but vanished.

"Don't you have your coat on yet, Paul?" she asked impatiently. "You know it upsets me to be late on mornings when I'm singing."

Dr. Herbert pulled his stiffened body out of the chair and picked up his coat. Taking his wife by the arm, he guided her to the front door. It was a nice morning for a drive anyway, he thought, knowing that before they had gone two blocks Frieda would have forgotten about going to church.

* * *

Grace Bible Church stood on the corner of Third and Elm. The recently completed sanctuary with its fifty-foot tower set the buildings distinctly apart from the small stores and apartments of the neighborhood. Directly west of the church was a vacant lot, already designated for future expansion, and beyond the lot a concrete-block home which served as the parsonage. Grace Church had grown in size and fervor over the past five years under Pastor McCormick's ministry, and Joyce Stoddard, standing across the street viewing the structure, uttered a silent vow of thanksgiving for what this church had meant in her own life. She remained on the corner, although the light had changed twice, still somewhat hesitant about taking her personal problems and laying them upon the McCormick's doorstep. Since she had already phoned, however, it was obviously a little late for a change of mind. When the light again turned green, she eased Danny's stroller off the curb and the two of them crossed the street, protected from the impatience of the midmorning traffic. Mother and son moved slowly down the sidewalk, past church and lot, and turned up the front walk of the parsonage. Joyce stooped over and lifted Danny from the stroller—a struggle that was becoming more difficult as he continued to grow. Carrying him up the steps, she rang the bell.

Katy McCormick answered the door with her customary smile. "Joyce! I'm so glad you could come over. Come on in." She beckoned Joyce to follow, and they passed through the living room into the sunny kitchen. The church had provided a good home for the McCormicks. Joyce viewed the birch cupboards

and built-in range with admiration. Café curtains of blue ging-
ham and a matching tablecloth in the dinette area produced a
woman's-magazine image, and the contrast with her own
gloomy breakfast nook couldn't have been more obvious.

"You like it?" asked Katy, turning the fire on under the coffee.

"It's lovely," replied Joyce. "I didn't know churches did so
well by their pastors."

Katy laughed heartily. "They don't always. You should
have seen the place we had back in Kansas!" She shook her
head, still smiling. "But we're grateful to the Lord for the gen-
erosity of the people here, and we'll enjoy it while it's ours.
Say there, Danny, let's see if we can find something for you to
play with."

Danny eagerly followed Mrs. McCormick into the next room,
and Joyce slipped into one of the chairs by the table. Her ap-
preciation for the decor of the kitchen was enhanced by the spot-
less and polished tile on the floor and the gleaming sink devoid
of dishes. Conscience reminded her of the pots and pans floating
in greasy water at home. Danny pranced back into the room
carrying a monkey fashioned from stuffed socks, and Katy
placed a box of assorted toys on the floor in front of him.

"Mine are a little past this stage, but we keep a collection
around for company." She busied herself with cups and saucers
and emptied the contents of a cookie jar onto a plate. "Bill will
be over in a minute. He's been painting in the annex this morning and will be glad to take a break."

"I—I hope I haven't upset your schedule or anything by coming over like this," Joyce stammered.

"Of course not," the pastor's wife insisted warmly. "We'll
start worrying when no one wants to come over to talk."

The back door swung open, and a man of medium build and
attired in painting overalls made an appearance. His hair was
prematurely grayed, but the deep-set and sparkling brown eyes
added a touch of youth to the face.

"Hi there, big man!" he greeted Danny while picking him up

and tossing him in the air. The little fellow squealed with delight. "Morning, Mrs. Stoddard." The pastor shook hands with Joyce. "Please excuse this outfit, but even preachers have to work for a living occasionally."

He took a seat opposite her, and Mrs. McCormick poured the coffee and carried it from the counter. Returning for the cookies, she handed one to the contented Danny, and then joined them at the table.

Pastor McCormick looked at the fare. "Worth thirty-five cents?" He grinned at his wife. Then he bowed his head and prayed, "Our gracious and loving Father, we thank Thee for Thy provision for our daily needs, and for Thy love and understanding for our daily problems. Bless this refreshment and our conversation. In Jesus' name. Amen."

"I forgot to ask if you were a coffee drinker," said Mrs. McCormick apologetically.

"Oh, yes," replied Joyce, adding generous amounts of cream and sugar.

"You're old enough, huh?" teased the pastor, and Joyce blushed. "I'm sorry," he added kindly, "that wasn't very nice."

Joyce forgot her earlier hesitancy in the presence of this warmhearted pair. In minutes she had felt more at home in their company than she usually was with her own parents.

"I understand that you wanted to talk to us about something," Pastor McCormick continued. He was not a man to waste time in small talk or purposeless activities and disliked sitting still for long periods of time.

"Yes," answered Joyce, encouraged by his straightforward approach. "I suppose this is something I could talk over with my folks, but I thought you might understand better. It's about my husband, Al. He's not a Christian, you know." They nodded their acknowledgment. "I guess you know that we had to get married two years ago, and my folks still haven't really forgiven him for that—at least I don't feel like they have. Anyway, that's all past now, and God used it to bring me to Him and to bring my parents back into the right sort of fellowship too, and I'm thankful for it. I really am." She stopped and took a sip of coffee. The McCormicks waited, watching her troubled young face. "Pastor," she continued seriously, "I want Al to know Christ, more than anything, but our marriage seems to be driving him away instead of closer. It's my fault in so many ways, and I'm just beginning to understand this. He's unhappy and restless and wishes he still was footloose and fancy-free like the rest of the guys he knows. I don't want our marriage to fall apart." Her voice cracked and tears crept into the corners of her eyes.

Pastor McCormick looked at her sympathetically. "Joyce, we can understand this. Whatever mistakes you have made cannot be undone, but the Lord intends that we go on from where we are. You have said yourself that He has worked a miracle in your life and in that of your parents, and we can surely pray that He might use this to touch Al's life as well. The consistency of your life in Christ as lived before your husband will doubtless have greater effect than anything you can say."

"I know this," Joyce answered quietly. "The Lord has been showing areas to me in the last few weeks where my life hasn't matched up with what I've said. But it's so hard to know what to do sometimes."

"What is it in particular that's bothering you now?"

"Well, I know I haven't made our apartment the kind of place Al is happy to come home to; so last night I suggested that he invite some of his friends over Friday evening. They're kind of a wild bunch, but they are his friends, and he was really excited about the idea. Then this morning he told me to be sure to have plenty of beer on hand for them. Can I do that, Pastor, as a Christian, I mean? Should I do it?"

Reverend McCormick rested his chin on a paint-spattered hand and quietly considered what had been said. He looked over at his wife whose face gave no indication of what she might be thinking. "Well, Joyce," he said at length, "there are several things involved here. First of all the Scriptures clearly teach that you are to be in subjection to your husband, regardless of his spiritual condition. So that if he wishes to serve liquor in his home, in spite of your feelings and objections, there is not much you can do about it. We must also remember that we cannot impose our Christian convictions upon those outside of Christ."

"Then you think I ought to just go along with him?"

He smiled. "Not so fast. Remember I said there are several things involved. Have you really talked this over with Al and explained to him why you'd rather not serve beer?"

"Well—not exactly." Joyce hesitated.

"I think that's the first step. More marriages suffer from a breakdown in communications than almost any other cause. Tell him how you feel. Ask him if his friends could go without their beer for one evening, or maybe they could have it after they leave your place."

"And suppose he won't go along with it?"

"Then let him be the one who buys it and serves it so that your own testimony is not affected."

Joyce studied the few coffee grounds in the bottom of her cup, her dark eyes serious and troubled beyond their years. "I'll try," she said, forcing a half smile.

"Good for you," he replied. "Let's talk to the Lord about it, and then I've got to get back to work."

The three figures sat with bowed heads around the little table. Joyce felt wonderfully uplifted and encouraged as the pastor's resonant voice poured out her needs to a concerned and loving God. *If only Al and I could have a home like this,* she thought. *If only—*

* * *

Marty pushed the bulky humanities text aside and laid her head on the pillow. She had been reading ever since dinner, and the words had begun to blur before her eyes. Lifting her head a little, she noticed with distaste that Jeanne's bed was inundated with two changes of clothes and a stack of books.

Marty wondered aloud why her roommate didn't put those books to use once in a while, especially with the first big test on tap tomorrow. Living with Jeanne was becoming more and more difficult to look at as a temporary thing not worth getting bothered about. The giggling and incessant munching that went on in that room were wearing on Marty's nerves. *Maybe I can get home this weekend,* she thought hopefully.

The door flew open, and Jeanne ducked quickly inside, slamming it behind her. Several loud thumps echoed from the hall, and then another door slammed.

"Hi!" she greeted Marty. "That nutty Corrine chased me clear down the hall with a wet towel, all because I just—"

"When are you guys going to grow up?" Marty interrupted. "No kidding, you're supposed to be in college now, but you act like a bunch of eight-year-olds."

Jeanne pushed aside some of the clutter on her bed and plopped down. Her face showed the sting of Marty's rebuke and, thoroughly chastened, she lamely ventured, "We were just having fun."

Marty watched her, puzzled as usual. It was impossible to say anything to this girl without her taking it terribly seriously. However, now that they were started, she might as well unload a few other suggestions. "Have you started studying for the humanities test?"

"Not yet," Jeanne replied, looking at her watch and frowning. "How come you're working so hard? You've had all A's on the quizzes."

Marty sat up and swung her legs onto the floor. "Because, my friend, I not only have to learn what's required at this dump, but also I've got to learn enough so that I won't be hopelessly behind at State next semester."

"You're still planning on that, huh?"

"You're right," Marty answered, getting up and walking over to her desk. "And I have to leave time to correct these papers this evening so I can earn the money to get me there."

"We all have to be at the dorm meeting in ten minutes."

Marty muttered her reaction under her breath. She turned to Jeanne with exasperation. "Would anyone miss me if I stayed up here?"

"The last time you tried it, Mrs. Dickenson came up after you," Jeanne reminded her.

"OK," conceded Marty, knowing it was useless to try to beat the rules at Coastal. "Maybe it won't last too long. What's it all about anyway?"

Jeanne shrugged her shoulders and picked up a book. Living with Marty was surely a cross to bear, and nothing like the Christian fellowship she had anticipated finding at Bible school. She brushed aside these momentary pangs of self-pity, but wondered if, and how, God could use her in the life of the sharp-looking but confused-thinking girl now seated at the desk thumbing through a stack of papers. Flipping a few pages in the thick book, her thoughts drifted back to the coincidental meeting with Pete after supper. At least he thought it was a coincidence.

"I was talking to Pete tonight," she commented in her most matter-of-fact manner.

"Great," said Marty flatly, displeased at further interruption.

"Come on, Marty," Jeanne said, bouncing off the bed and dragging a chair over to her roommate's side. "Can't you admit that Pete's just a little bit terrific?"

"You and Corrine!" she replied, shaking her head.

"I don't think about him like Corrine!" Jeanne defended herself at this superinsult. "I mean as a friend. He just knows so much and is so wise in spiritual things. I wish you could talk to him sometime."

Marty laid her pen down and sat back in the chair. Jeanne was treading on dangerous ground again, and one of these days she was going to go too far. "I don't need help and counsel from Pete Bradley or anyone else around this place." Her voice was even but tinged with impatience. "And you'd better find another victim for your interests, Jeanne, or you and I aren't going to last even one semester in the same room. OK?"

Jeanne pulled the chair back to her own desk. "Sorry," she replied quietly. "Guess I'll go on downstairs for the meeting."

Marty sighed and, desiring to restore whatever harmony possible to the situation, got to her feet. "Wait till I get my robe, and I'll go with you."

Jeanne smiled with relief that no permanent breach had been made, and the two girls went out into the hall together. The corridor of the upper floor of Cullen Hall, the only girls' dormitory on campus, was lighted by a series of overhead lamps which cast eerie shadows on the wooden-plank walls. Cullen, like the other main buildings at Coastal, had been constructed as a part of Central State Boys' Reformatory. To Marty, this connection with the previous occupants was ironically appropriate. Though the boys and their keepers had been transferred to a new location years ago, the buildings had proven durable, and a few coats of paint and a minimum of remodeling had transformed the site into a home for a Bible school. The somewhat ragged history of Coastal was known to most of the students, but financially, at least, the school now appeared able to stand on its own. Cullen Hall's lower level contained a large and comfortable lounge. The furnishings were such that no one worried about putting their feet on them, and it served as a center for discussions and diversions.

Spotting a vacant chair, Jeanne dashed for it and then motioned for Marty to join her. Marty perched on the arm, surveying the already crowded room from a safe distance. She was aware that most of the students had written her off as being aloof and conceited, but she was happy to stay clear of any involvement. Mrs. Dickenson paced nervously at one end of the room. She was an attractive, silver-haired woman in her late fifties. Under other circumstances Marty might have found the housemother a congenial acquaintance; as it was, they had become dedicated foes in a matter of a few weeks. When it appeared that all of the stragglers had arrived, Mrs. Dickenson whipped out her infamous blue notebook and disappeared down the hall.

"Sherlock Holmes on a fresh trail," Marty whispered to Jeanne.

Annette Perkins, a willowy, blonde senior and a lit major, took a position behind the small table at the front of the room. Marty had categorized Annette and her pal, Barbara Sheldon, as the two biggest hypocrites she had met at Coastal thus far. They had their hands in everything that went on and served as ruthless dictators, all within the protective custody of spiritual cliques.

"We don't want to keep you girls long tonight," Annette began. "I know some of you have tests tomorrow, and we also want to leave time for a season of prayer after we've finished with the business on hand."

Barbara Sheldon nodded her solemn agreement, and Marty felt like gagging.

"We have received permission from the administration to hold an open house here at the dorm tomorrow night. Those of you who were at school last year will remember the good times of Christian fellowship we had on these occasions, and I personally am burdened that we show some of the newer students at Coastal the real joy that can be found in the simple pleasures done in our Lord's name. To refresh your memories, at an open house we invite the fellows to join us for an evening of table games followed by a time of singing and refreshments. You don't need to have a date to come, and we want a real fine turnout. Now if I could have volunteers for a committee to organize the games, and another to be in charge of preparing the food—"

"Big deal," Marty muttered, happy to have baby-sitting duties with Mrs. Herbert scheduled for Friday evening.

* * *

"I don't know, Joyce." Al rubbed a massive hand through his kinky black hair, "Those guys don't know how to have a party without anything to drink! What would we do all evening?"

"Can't we drink cokes, listen to records, talk—I don't know exactly, but it shouldn't be that hard to find something to do."

He looked skeptical, but finally shrugged his shoulders. "OK," he reluctantly agreed, "we'll do it your way."

She kissed his forehead and returned to the kitchen to test the newly waxed floor.

* * *

It was a little past seven when Marty arrived at the Herberts. She had applied for the job as Mrs. Herbert's "companion" on her first day at Coastal, and this had opened up an opportunity to correct papers for Dr. Herbert's first-year German class. It would have made a wonderful testimony for an answer to prayer, thought Marty, except for the fact that she hadn't done any praying! Amused at her own observations, she chuckled softly and rang the bell.

"Come in, Martha." Dr. Herbert grasped her hand warmly and led her into the front room. "I'm sorry to take you away from the dorm party tonight, but I've had this speaking engagement for several months."

"That's all right. I'd rather be here anyway. Where's Mrs. Herbert?"

"She went to bed right after supper, and I would imagine she's asleep for the night. You're welcome to study or read or whatever you wish." He thought of mentioning the unwashed dishes, but decided against it.

"I can't take money for doing nothing, Dr. Herbert. Have you got some ironing or cleaning that needs to be done?"

"Well," he hesitated, "the kitchen is rather a mess, if you're sure you don't mind."

"I've had lots of practice with messy kitchens at home." Marty grinned.

"It's very sweet of you," he said, picking up his battered briefcase. "I should be back in a couple of hours."

Marty watched through the front window until the professor's car pulled out of the driveway. She walked slowly into the kitchen and shook her head at the remnants of several meals left on the table and stove. She wouldn't have agreed to the extra work for just anyone, but the doctor and his wife were the most decent people she had met since leaving Santa Alberta. Marty hadn't been kidding about having had practice. She laughingly reminisced about the times she had been stuck with the dishes while Joyce had run off to some kind of a meeting or get-together. Of course it hadn't seemed very funny then.

Life has a way of making things even though, and Joyce was finally getting her share of housework. Marty tossed these random thoughts around in her mind, playing with the idea of justice meted out by life itself for a while, but unable to forget entirely the letter she had received from Molly Bergan that morning. It hadn't really been much of a letter—two sides of flowered notepaper. Enough, however, to let her know that Richie was keeping steady company with a girl in Molly's pledge class. Marty had known it was inevitable, though she had hoped that he wouldn't forget quite so quickly. Patting the edge of the sink methodically with a soapy hand, the hard lines of determination formed around her mouth. It was just one more reason, as if she really needed any more, why she had to get out of this place by next semester.

When the last of the pots and pans had been dipped thoroughly in the rinse water and at least the top layer of scum wiped from the stove, Marty dried her hands and walked into the front room. She peeked around the corner into the bedroom and observed that Mrs. Herbert was dozing peacefully. *In spite of her snowy white hair, she looks like a child,* thought Marty.

The doorbell rang, but the old woman slept on undisturbed. Marty crossed to the entry hall, curious as to who would call on the Herberts at this hour. She opened the door and stepped back with surprise.

"What are you doing here?" she questioned, somewhat flustered.

Pete Bradley's blue eyes twinkled as he obviously enjoyed her sudden lack of poise. "I've brought back some books I borrowed from Doc."

"He's not here this evening."

"I know. May I come in long enough to put them back in the bookcase?"

"Of course," Marty replied coldly. She was disgusted with herself for letting him upset her.

Pete came inside, and Marty closed the door behind him. He strolled leisurely and confidently to the scarred oak bookcase in the corner and replaced the books he had been carrying. She watched him hunch down to look at two volumes on the bottom shelf. He flipped the pages slowly, put these down on the floor and removed another. Marty stood by the door with growing impatience. She didn't share her roommate's admiration for the conceited king of Coastal's spiritual life. *Real Christian humility,* she reflected bitterly. *Thinks he has all the answers!* Deciding to ignore his intrusion, especially since he was doing such a good job of ignoring her presence, she started for the kitchen.

"I have a paper due in theology Monday," he said, matter-of-factly getting up from the floor to sit down on the couch. "Need to finish the first draft tonight, so if I'm not bothering you too much I'd like to check Chafer's views while I'm here."

"Go ahead," she answered, maintaining the same unconcerned tone he had used.

He took some three-by-five-inch cards out of his pocket and began making notes. Marty's better judgment told her to go on into the kitchen and busy herself with something until he left, but curiosity impelled her to sit down on one of the straight-backed chairs by the dining table and watch. She recognized that there was something about him that interested her, though she didn't know what it was, and the thought of becoming a partner in Jeanne's fan club repelled her. He was not especially good-looking, at least not by her standards, but he had an air of confidence that separated him from the rest of the fellows on campus. Marty had thought many times that if these guys were really so sold on what they believed that they ought to stand up and be proud of it instead of being so mousey and apologetic.

"Too bad you're missing the party," he said, looking up.

"You aren't there either," she returned.

"Would be if I could."

"That paper couldn't wait till tomorrow?" she asked, sensing that she had caught him in a bit of obvious hypocrisy.

"I work twelve hours on Saturdays."

"You still have all day Sunday."

Pete closed the book and smiled. It was a contagious little-boy sort of smile, and Marty's heart beat faster, much to her own surprise. "You probably don't see it this way," he said, "but I figure that Sunday is the Lord's day. And if I've wasted my study time at parties during the week, it still doesn't give me the right to cheat Him out of His day."

If Jeanne had made a pious statement like that, Marty would have wasted no time in cutting her down with a reminder that the "law" had been done away. With Pete, however, she hesitated, suspecting that he might be sincere, and doubting that she would come out ahead in any exchange of smart remarks anyway. "Everybody to his own way of thinking, I guess." She wished that he would pack up his books and go home.

"And what's your way of thinking?"

"About what?" she asked, caught off-balance again.

"Oh, about life, and about the Lord, and the school—"

"You've been talking to my roommate, haven't you?" she countered, now on the defensive.

"A little," he answered. "But then, you haven't tried to keep your feelings much of a secret."

"Then you shouldn't have to ask." Marty was angry. The conversation had turned into the same kind of cross-examination that she received regularly from Jeanne and the others in the dorm.

Pete was still smiling and sitting comfortably on the couch. "Just thought maybe you could tell me why you're so bitter about Christianity. Do you know the Lord, Marty?"

"I know all I want to know about churches and religion," she answered hastily. Her face flushed and the words came out too quickly.

"What made you come to Coastal then?"

"It wasn't any 'what,' it was 'who.' My parents insisted that I come."

Pete nodded his head with understanding and looked down at the floor. Marty waited for the expected sermon, but it didn't come. Instead he gathered up his collection of books and notes and started for the door.

"Don't misunderstand," she said, quickly following him. For the first time she felt somewhat guilty about having expressed her opinion. "I'm not really bitter about Christianity. I don't mind going to church, and I believe in God and all that. It's just—well, I resent being made to stay here where everybody is so—well, fanatical about church things." She watched his expression, hoping that she had made herself clear because, surprisingly, it seemed to matter.

"I don't blame you," he said quietly. "If I didn't know Christ personally, I think I'd hate this place too. Good night, Marty."

"Good night," she replied as he went down the front steps. Reluctantly she closed the door and leaned against it. At last she laughed—laughed at the serious but misguided young man whose car was pulling out of the drive, and laughed at herself for getting so wrought up in his presence. *He must have something,* she thought and then laughed again. *You're losing your cool, baby,* she said half aloud. *You need to get away from this fruity place!* She was glad to be going home tomorrow; even a couple of days would help. At the same time she hoped she would have a chance to talk to Pete again. Life could be so confusing sometimes.

*   *   *

Joyce patted one of the sofa pillows and propped it in the corner, covering, she hoped, the worst of the sags in the cushion. The apartment was strangely quiet without Danny. Except for the queasy feeling she had been having in her stomach for two days, Joyce felt as young and carefree as she ever had. It would be good to spend time with other kids their own age; somehow in the seriousness of the past year they had gotten away from their own age group.

"Sit down, will ya? It makes me nervous to watch you walking around." Al dropped the newspaper he had just finished beside the chair, but his wife's anguished look condemned him. "OK, OK," he muttered, taking the paper out to the kitchen wastebasket.

"Does everything look all right?" Joyce asked hesitantly as he returned.

"Sure, it's fine," he replied with a rare showing of compassion. "Don't worry so much, doll—they probably won't stay very long anyway."

The buzzer sounded, and Al went to the door. A group of men and women in their early twenties stood in the hall. The self-appointed leader of the crowd was a tall, dark-haired fellow with a conceited expression. He was older than the others, confident to the point of cockiness, and he placed his hand on Al's broad shoulder as he came inside.

"Right on time—just like I promised." He was speaking to Al, but his eyes were professionally appraising Joyce. A half smile formed on his lips and he nodded his approval.

"Glad you could make it, Bud." Al shut the door when the

last of the gang had trooped in. "Joyce, this is Bud Bailey, our coach—my wife, Joyce."

Bud walked over until he was standing directly in front of Joyce. Feet planted wide apart and hands in his pockets, he stood relaxed, enjoying her evident discomfort. "Al ought to bring you out to watch us play—it's not fair to keep something this good all to himself!"

Al introduced her to the other members of the team and their dates. She remembered some of the fellows as having been a few years ahead of her in high school. The girls were all strangers and carried a certain uniformity of attitude and approach that she was self-consciously certain she no longer possessed. "Sit down," Al gestured to the group as a whole. With an indication of his head he directed Joyce to the kitchen. She excused herself and disappeared into the other room, feeling strangely flustered and confused, and not knowing why. The refrigerator contained a variety of cold pop and some sandwiches she had made before taking Danny over to her mother's that afternoon. She set these out on a large pink-flowered tray. It had been used only a couple of times since their marriage, but in spite of its impracticality the tray held the distinction of having been the only store-wrapped and delivered wedding present they had received. Marty had felt this was a required gesture and Joyce had accepted the gift gracefully, knowing that it represented whatever was left of her sister's love and admiration.

"Joyce!" Al called. "What are you doin' in there?"

Al wasn't so sure of himself this evening either, she acknowledged while opening a bag of potato chips. Hoping that she had fixed neither too much nor too little in the way of refreshments, Joyce returned to the living room carrying the tray. Bud hopped to his feet to assist her.

"A real feast," he commented, setting the food down on the somewhat wobbly coffee table. "Maybe you could give Pam here some lessons." Bud's voice had a touch of sarcasm which Joyce didn't comprehend, but it was evident that the sleepy-

eyed blonde at his side had gotten the message. Her lower lip
curled with disdain and she leaned over to mumble something
in his ear. Bud threw his head back and laughed, and the girl
slapped his face. She walked over to the window and peered
through the curtains into the night.

Bud's dark eyes flashed, but the lopsided grin remained. "My
woman doesn't appreciate me, Joyce. I'll bet you don't treat
Al that way, do you?"

Joyce looked over at her husband, who did not appear concerned about all the attention she was getting, in fact, he had
a satisfied and almost proud expression on his broad face.

"Dig in," Al directed the others, who had not been bothered
either by the short dramatic scene nor by the exchange of looks
between husband and wife. Pam abandoned her station at the
window and sat down beside Al, still pouting and petulant.
Finding a chair, Joyce sank down and tried to assess the situation. She had worried all day about what to do for entertainment, but this concern had obviously been unfounded since conversation and joking proceeded naturally. Bud sat on the floor in
the center of what had become a circle, and Joyce began to sense
why Al had complained of being left out. Stories were being
told with allusions to other events or other stories; sentences
were often only half finished; yet the bond of understanding
seemed to cover the gaps, and reactions came on cue. Joyce
watched with a growing feeling that this partytime atmosphere
was something that could be turned on or off at will. She sat
apart as a spectator—an outsider.

"That's right, isn't it, Mrs. Stoddard?"

Joyce suddenly realized that Bud was speaking to her and
that she had unknowingly become an object of interest.

She smiled. "I'm sorry, I didn't hear what you said."

Laughter echoed throughout the room, but Bud rose from
his place of prominence and came over to where she was sitting.
"Don't mind these dogs; tell me all about you. What do you do
all day for excitement?" His eyes were serious and his voice

intent, but the beginnings of a smile at the corner of his mouth
left Joyce uncertain as to whether or not this was a game or an
honest inquiry.

She was spared the task of answering when Pam stood up
and stated loudly, "I'm thirsty for something besides root beer!"

Two of the fellows who had been lounging in front of the
darkened TV agreed.

"How 'bout it, Bud?"

He looked at Joyce, framing the question without words.
She shook her head.

"We could go down to Harry's on the corner—my treat all
around," interjected Al, eager to please.

"Sounds all right by me," Bud replied. "You coming with
us?" he asked Joyce.

"No, I need to pick up the baby at my mother's."

He shrugged his shoulders, and the others drifted into the
bedroom to collect sweaters and jackets. As quickly as they
had arrived and fallen into place, the group vanished, leaving
only the traces of empty bottles and a few crumbs on the rug.
Al had found a spot in the regiment and had disappeared without any particular word to his wife.

He's a part of them now, Joyce mused, pushing the chairs
back around the table. *And that must mean the "party" was a
success.* She laughed quietly, but it was a sick attempt at humor
for she knew that she was neither able nor wished to belong.
Tears pushed their way into her eyes; her uneasy stomach turned
over in rebellion at the same time. Joyce Miller Stoddard,
twenty years old, white, female, ex-cheerleader, ex-junior-prom
queen, ex-everything, hurried for the bathroom.

*   *   *

It was four o'clock in the afternoon before Marty even
thought about calling her sister. She had caught a ride with
two fellows from nearby Creston who would take her back the
next evening. They hadn't proven very interesting traveling
companions, and Marty had been relieved to see the familiar

streets of Santa Alberta. After basking in the surprised and receptive homecoming from her parents, Marty had sneaked away to her own room and caught up on several hours of sleep. Now, rested and relaxed from a leisurely, uninterrupted tub bath, she sought out her mother's company, expecting and receiving the attention always due a returned hero.

"You ought to let Joyce know you're here," Mrs. Miller counseled. "I know she'll be anxious to hear about what you've been doing."

"Maybe I'll just take the car and go over and surprise her."

Her mother hesitated. "I don't know whether Al's home or not."

"What difference does that make?" Marty retorted. "Al doesn't bite." Her mother reached for her purse and, after a moment's searching, handed over the keys to the Chevy. "You'll be back for supper, won't you?"

"Sure," Marty replied. "I want to call a couple of kids and see if we can't catch a show tonight."

Her mother's face dropped noticeably. Marty wasn't sure whether it was because she wasn't spending enough time at home or because Coastal hadn't cured her of a normal interest in a good movie. Whatever the reason, Marty disappeared out the back door before having to listen to any sermon on the subject.

It was a pleasantly warm Indian-summer afternoon. Joyce and Al's apartment was on the south side of Santa Alberta, and Marty enjoyed cruising through the traffic. She was in no particular hurry, in fact, not even particularly anxious to visit with her older sister. It would be fun to get Joyce riled up by telling her about all the creeps who inhabited Coastal, but otherwise there wasn't much to talk about. It would be a chance to call Molly and find out more about Richie. At home her mother's "interest and concern" always included eavesdropping on telephone conversations and, if Richie was really gone on some other girl, Marty could do without her mother's insincere con-

solation. She pulled up in front of the large brick building, set
the brake, and got out. Al's car was missing from its usual
place in the adjoining lot, so Marty figured to have no run-ins
with her uncouth brother-in-law. *Spare me from anything like
Al—ever,* she thought, going inside and up the stairs.

Joyce answered the door. "Come in, stranger!" she said, surprised and pleased. "What are you doing around these parts?"

"The warden gave me a weekend off for good behavior."
Marty grinned, following her sister into the front room. Danny
was corralled in the playpen eating a graham cracker, most of
which was either on his face or the front of his shirt. Marty
pushed aside a pile of clothes on the couch and sat down. Her
nephew gave no signs of remembering her, so she gave him the
same treatment.

"Sorry about the mess," Joyce apologized. "Danny and I just
got back from the laundromat."

"It's OK—my roommate's half of our room always looks
like this!" She looked around. "Where's Al today?"

"He went bowling with some of the fellows."

Marty sniffed, making no attempt to hide her distaste. "Same
old Al, huh?"

Joyce didn't answer, and Marty regretted the outspoken comment. "Well, how do I look? More 'spiritual' after four weeks
of chapel, Bible classes and prayer meetings?"

Her sister smiled indulgently.

"Did you notice I'm even acquiring the proper vocabulary?
The key to everything is being 'spiritual'—big deal, huh! At
Coastal you can goof off your studies, insult people to their
faces, ignore all sorts of basic decencies, anything—and as long
as it's connected with 'being spiritual,' you've got it made!"
Marty laughed without bitterness, enjoying her newly regained
sense of humor.

"You don't seem too hung up over it."

"Oh, it's about as bad as I expected, but I guess I'm learning
to live with it."

"Haven't you found anything good about the place though?" Joyce teased.

"Not much. Most of the kids are pure fakes, though I have met a couple of good guys along the way," she admitted.

"Coming from you, after only one month up there, I'd have to count that as encouraging!"

"Count it however you like," said Marty, continuing the banter. "I feel too good today to even knock good ol' Coastal very hard. Can I use your phone for a minute?" she asked, looking toward the kitchen.

"Help yourself."

Marty walked over to the wall phone by the stove and dialed a familiar number. "Mrs. Bergan? Is Molly there—Will she be home at all this weekend?—All right, thank you." She replaced the receiver and stood tapping her fingers on the wall trying to think of some other possible source of information.

"No luck?" said Joyce, carrying a wiggling Danny to the sink. She wiped off most of the wet-cracker remains and turned him loose with a pat on the seat of his baggy pants. He ran into the other room and plopped down on the floor with a self-accompanying "Boom!"

"He's learned a new word."

"Budding genius," commented Marty vaguely. She shrugged off her temporary disappointment over Molly and noticed her sister taking things out of the refrigerator.

"Can you stay for supper?"

"Sorry, promised Mom I'd be back."

"Want a coke or something? We've got plenty for a change." Joyce indicated a lower shelf packed with bottles.

"What have you been doing? Entertaining?"

"Uh-huh. Didn't Mom tell you?"

"No," Marty answered, selecting a cold bottle. "I really haven't had a chance to talk to Mom very much yet."

"Have you given her any chance to talk to you yet?" Joyce queried as they left the kitchen.

"Nope," Marty conceded, sitting down on the cluttered sofa again.

"Same old Marty."

They talked easily and lightly about a lot of things—much as they had always done in those years when they had shared both a bedroom and all personal secrets. Marty noted that her sister was pale in spite of all the animation.

"You feeling good, Joyce?"

"I've had a touch of stomach flu or something—otherwise A-OK."

"You never finished telling me about the entertaining or whatever you've been doing with all that pop."

"Oh, it wasn't anything so much. Some of Al's friends came over last night."

"I thought you couldn't stand Al's friends."

"I can't," she replied simply.

"The party must have been a big success then."

"Al thought it was. At least they asked him to go bowling with them today."

Marty shook her head and smiled wistfully. "It's kind of a big mess, isn't it, sis?"

"Kind of," Joyce agreed.

"I'm sorry things haven't turned out any better."

Joyce managed a grin. "Don't feel bad. I'm reaping a bit of what's been sown. I believe the Lord'll make it better in time."

Marty's attitude changed from pity to contempt. Joyce couldn't have more effectively shattered the mood if she had poured a bucket of ice water down her younger sister's back. "Sure, sure," she said, getting up to leave. "Just keep on being 'spiritual' and everything will turn out happy-dandy."

"You're right, little sis," Joyce said softly. "Whether you know it or not, you're right."

*　　*　　*

The beautiful weather of the weekend continued over into Monday. Marty Miller returned to school reluctantly. Al Stoddard went back to work in the hardware department in the basement of Santa Alberta's largest store, carrying with him a slight hangover and a slightly guilty conscience for having pushed his wife around the night before. In the office of Dr. Ralph B. Moran a cluster of well-dressed women waited their turn.

"Mrs. Stoddard?"

"Yes," Joyce acknowledged, getting up from a Danish-modern settee in the corner.

"Right this way." The nurse led her past the main desk and down a short corridor. "Let's check your weight," she said pleasantly and indicated the scales. Joyce slipped off her shoes and obediently got on.

"One hundred fourteen," observed the nurse. "Wish all our patients were that careful!" She popped a thermometer into Joyce's mouth. "Now, if you'll help me with this preliminary information form—"

Joyce mumbled the replies, wondering why medical personnel always combined questioning and temperature-taking in one activity.

"Well," commented the nurse, repeating her ingratiating smile, "it all sounds very promising. If you'll just take a seat in this waiting room, Dr. Moran will be with you shortly."

Promising? thought Joyce sadly. She entered the small room where the nurse had pointed. It was crowded. Most of the other women were reading and barely glanced up to acknowledge the presence of a newcomer. All of them were wearing maternity clothes.

This is probably the waiting room for another waiting room, reflected Joyce, aware of Dr. Moran's reputation. She had thought about going to the clinic, but had finally decided that she was less apt to meet anyone she knew this way. The woman

seated in the next chair reached awkwardly to replace a magazine on the coffee table and then looked her way.

Joyce brushed a wisp of hair away from her eye, carefully
displaying the gold band on her fourth finger.

The woman cleared her throat. "Your first?" she asked, taking a cigarette out of her purse.

"No."

The woman, annoyed at having misjudged the situation, continued inanely, "You have other children at home?"

"Yes," Joyce replied, wishing that her new-found friend
would pick up another magazine.

"My goodness," the woman said to no one in particular,
"people are certainly starting their families young these days!"

Joyce didn't answer. She leaned back and closed her eyes,
and her companion turned her attention on another neighbor.
Aided by the soft music which filtered in from unseen speakers,
Joyce let her thoughts drift away from the bulky ladies and the
antiseptic office aroma. It seemed that complications were coming more quickly than she could handle them. She ruefully re-
called her confident assurances to Marty a few days earlier and
sought to regain the peace she had felt then. It wasn't to be
found, and she wished she were somewhere else, doing something else, feeling some way else— At least Dr. Moran could
tell her for certain, and she had to be absolutely sure before
saying anything to Al. *When Al comes home tonight,* she
thought and then mentally corrected herself, *if Al comes home
tonight*— Joyce shook her head and sighed audibly. The lady
on her left looked around again.

"Mrs. Riley?" The nurse stuck her head in the door and
beckoned to a red-haired woman.

If Al comes home. Joyce shut her eyes once more. *He's got
to come home tonight—he's got to!* Her private world whirled
with problems that were beyond her scope and understanding.

It was nearly six that evening when the door of the apartment slammed. From the bedroom where she was changing Danny's diaper, Joyce called out, "Is that you, Al?"

"You expecting somebody more interesting?"

She heard the refrigerator door close and then the clatter of the lid on the electric skillet. Picking Danny up from the bed, she hurried out through the living room. Al was standing in the curtained archway that led to the kitchen.

"How come all the fancy food?" he grumbled.

She brushed past him and pushed Danny into the high chair. Fumbling, trying to snap on the tray that never had worked, she managed to reply just a little too brightly, "I just thought we could have something special for dinner, and afterward maybe we could take a walk or something."

"What would we do with him?" he asked, coming up behind her and placing his arms around her waist.

"I could ask Mrs. Shea across the hall to listen for him." Her heart sank as he leaned his head down upon her shoulder; he had been drinking.

"Well, I'm not hungry and my feet are killing me already, so let's forget the whole thing." He pushed her away and stumbled into the other room.

Handing the baby a set of measuring spoons, Joyce followed him. "Come on, Al," she said, still trying. "You got paid today, didn't you? Let's celebrate!"

"I've already celebrated," he responded sullenly.

"Mama! Mama!" Danny fussed, unwilling to be left out of anything.

Joyce's lips tightened, and she struggled to hold control. "I know you've been celebrating," she said evenly. "I try to be deaf and blind to some things that go on, but it's hard to ignore what I can smell!"

"Bravo! Pretty speech!" The lines around his mouth were hard. "You want to know how much of the paycheck I spent so far? Huh?"

"No," said Joyce.

"Aw, come on. It'll give you an excuse to blow up as big as you did last night!" He goaded her with sarcasm.

"Al, I went to the doctor this morning."

"Why?" he asked, suddenly concerned. "I didn't really hurt you, did I?"

"I wanted to find out if I was pregnant again."

He stepped back, stunned. "Well—"

Joyce nodded wearily.

Al stared at her, unbelieving, and then slowly the anger kindled in his dark eyes. "You stupid woman!" He said the words emphatically, and looked around the room, wildly clutching for some kind of straw. "Boy, this is it! This is really it!"

Joyce was startled by this abrupt reaction. She had expected him to get mad, but she had never seen Al quite like this before.

"Mama!" wailed Danny from the kitchen.

Al picked up the jacket he had thrown over the back of the chair.

"You're not going out again?" she challenged.

"I'm through, Joyce. I'm really through!" he sputtered. "Maybe you think having babies and playing house is fun, but I've had it! I want out!"

"Stop shouting at me!"

"Listen to me, Joyce." His voice became calm again and the anguished expression faded. There was certainty in his manner as he spoke. "I want you to listen and this time I want you to understand. It was a mistake that we ever got married in the first place, and everything we've done since then has just been piling more mistakes on top of the first one. You've turned into a religious nut, and I'm nothing but a stinkin' drunk anymore. Let's call it quits, huh baby? Before it gets any worse!"

Joyce couldn't believe it was really happening. "You don't mean that?" she asked quietly, too shocked to release the flood of emotion inside her.

"I'm sorry, Joycie, I really do." He walked past her into the bedroom.

"What are you going to do?" She was suddenly panicked.

"Just get a few things," he replied, reaching for a suitcase on the closet shelf.

"You can't walk out on me like this!" she cried with disbelief. "What about Danny?"

"I'm sorry about Danny—this new one too."

"Sorry?" she exclaimed. "What good does 'sorry' do?" Her voice cracked, and she collapsed on the bed in tears.

Al finished cleaning out the dresser drawer. He grabbed a couple of shirts from hangers, stuffed them in the suitcase and snapped the lid shut. Pausing a moment to look at the sobbing dark-haired figure on the bed, he took a deep breath and left the room.

"Al?" Joyce called out, propping herself up on one elbow. "Al?" The front door slammed.

"Al!!" she screamed.

"Mama! Mama!"

3

Jeanne

CALEB J. HARRISON'S PORTRAIT hung above the fireplace in the lounge of the main building, his austere expression adding a touch of dignity to an otherwise drably furnished room. The individual stacks of books left on tables or in corners indicated that the dinner hour was still in progress, though small groups of students were beginning to trail in from the main hallway.

Jeanne Robbins had been seated on a sofa near the side door for ten minutes. She had rushed through her meal, even skipping the dessert—a considerable personal sacrifice for her—in order to be among the first to reach the lounge. The denim-covered notebook with "Bradley" stenciled on the front and the two thick texts were still neatly stacked on the mantel, and she intended to wait patiently until the owner returned to claim them. She wished vaguely that someone else would sit down with her so that she would be less conspicuous. It would be especially fine if Bobby Jordan, the six-foot-four-inch prospective center for the basketball team, just happened to decide that his feet were weary and just happened to sit down next to her. Or even Fred Korinsky. He had spoken to her once when they were both at the mailboxes. Fred, however, continued to lean against the wall, probably waiting for someone, and Bobby never turned away from the crowd that surrounded him. Jeanne sighed, but quickly rationalized that a chance to talk to Pete was worth all the Freds and Bobbys put together.

There had been several occasions during these first two months of school for long conversations with Pete, not just the drippy moaning over upcoming tests that one usually heard on campus, but deep talks about spiritual matters. He even shared her concern for Marty's salvation, and Jeanne had been thrilled when he had made extra effort to be friendly to her roommate. Most of the kids left Marty alone, and she really couldn't blame them too much. Her roommate maintained a superior air, a straight A average, and a cool disdain for all regulations. Rumors had it that the dean of women, Miss Hawley, had called her in for a little "talk," but Marty hadn't mentioned it, and Jeanne had been afraid to ask.

At six-forty Pete Bradley entered the lounge. He seemed preoccupied and, without looking around, he gathered up his books and headed back into the hall. Quietly Jeanne slipped out the side door. According to her calculations, if she walked up the road to the dorm slowly he should be coming out just as she passed the main entrance of Harrison. She held her breath as the front door swung open and was rewarded by a glimpse of a wiry figure in a yellow-plaid shirt.

"Hi!" she called with mock surprise.

Pete looked up, grinned and waited for her to catch up. "How's it going?" he asked.

"Oh, I'm keeping pretty busy," she replied lightly.

"Worried about midterms tomorrow?"

"Not too much."

Pete laughed. "You and your roommate don't have much of anything in common, do you?"

"What makes you say that?"

"Just that she had a book propped up in front of her all through dinner."

"Did you eat dinner with Marty?" Jeanne asked with interest.

"Well, you could hardly say that I ate 'with' her. We were sitting at the same table."

"Did you get a chance to talk to her?"

"A little." Pete kicked a rock over to the side of the road. The graveled road carried traffic from the main gate past the boy's dorm, Harrison and the girls' dorm, in that order, ending in the downhill parking area to the rear of the campus. They were now walking in that direction.

"About spiritual things?" Jeanne asked anxiously.

"Not at a table full of other kids," he replied, and she thought there was a trace of impatience in his voice. "I don't think Marty needs any more 'talking to' anyway. She can't avoid hearing the gospel every day in classes and chapel."

"She skips chapel pretty often," Jeanne interjected.

He stopped in front of the women's dorm. "Don't you agree that she knows the plan of salvation already?"

"Oh, yes," she admitted quickly.

"Then I think we need to be praying that the Holy Spirit might use someone or something to convict her heart of her personal need for Christ. Arguing doesn't help the situation."

"No, I suppose not," she replied, regretting her obvious blunder. "I've been trying to get her interested in school activities—you know, like the sophomore banquet." Jeanne threw this last suggestion in casually and was astonished by her own bravery. The banquet was scheduled for a week from Friday and, though it was not necessarily a date affair, only a few rebels had ever gone by themselves. It was really too much to hope that Pete—but still—

"Is she interested in the banquet?" Pete asked with surprise.

"Oh, no," she replied hastily, hoping that he hadn't misunderstood. "She said she wouldn't go if someone paid her. Marty thinks all the guys on campus are drippy—even Bobby Jordan. Did you know he asked her out a couple of weeks ago, and she turned him down!"

Pete smiled again. "That's just as well. Jordan wouldn't do Marty any good."

"Isn't he saved either?" Jeanne's blue eyes were wide with surprise.

"He just has some problems," Pete answered with a finality that closed the matter. He looked at his watch. "I've got to pick up some things down at the station for Dr. Todd. See you later, Jeanne. Keep praying."

"Bye," she called with a half wave. She watched him for a moment, then strolled up the short walk to Cullen Hall.

"Boy, you must rate!" Corrine's booming voice cut into Jeanne's dream world. She turned with a start to find Corrine and Sally Hoving seated in the dilapidated hammock that hung on the wide front porch of the dormitory. Walking over to join them, Jeanne remarked calmly, "You mean Pete?"

"Did he walk you home?" asked Corrine intently.

"Well—yes."

"What were you talking about out there?"

"Take it easy, Corrine," Sally admonished.

"Yes, Corrine," Jeanne said, "there's nothing to get excited about. We were just talking about Bobby Jordan and the sophomore banquet and a lot of things."

"The sophomore banquet!" Corrine exploded. "Did he ask you to the sophomore banquet?"

"No, he just mentioned it," Jeanne answered, realizing in that instant that the truth was getting away from her a bit.

"Humph," said Corrine, getting up from her seat and going inside the building. Jeanne sat down beside Sally.

"It's a beautiful evening, isn't it?"

"I guess so," Sally responded without much enthusiasm. "I ought to be upstairs studying. Say, don't let Corrine bother you."

"Oh, I won't."

"Good. She's so far gone over Pete that she'd jump to any wild conclusion." Sally stood up and stretched. "If you see my roommate, tell her I'll be going up to the library about eight. OK?"

"OK," Jeanne answered softly, wondering why it was a "wild conclusion" to think that Pete might have asked her to the banquet. She swung the hammock lazily in the semidarkness as she thought about it.

*   *   *

Marty had intended to leave the library at five minutes to nine, but a last-second find in a reference book delayed her. It was actually three minutes after the hour when she reached the front door of Cullen, and she glanced about furtively for possible witnesses. There were none, and she hurriedly signed in for nine o'clock. Checking the lounge and finding it full, Marty decided to finish her English paper in her room. She bounded up the stairs, made the automatic turn to the right, counted three doors and opened the fourth.

Jeanne had been lying on the bed, and she sat up abruptly when Marty came in. Pushing a partially consumed bag of peanuts under the pillow, she croaked a hoarse, "Hi!"

"Hi," Marty mumbled in return. She dropped her load of books on the desk and then stared thoughtfully at her roommate. "What have you been doing all evening?"

"Oh, I've been studying. I just quit for a while to rest my eyes."

Marty nodded and observed that Jeanne's books were in a pile on the dresser. "Pleasant dreams?" she asked with a touch of sarcasm.

Jeanne reddened and said nothing.

Marty undressed quickly, only to remember with dismay that her robe was still hanging on the line outside.

"What's the matter?" Jeanne asked.

"I forgot about washing my robe—it's still wet."

"Wear mine. I'm not going to need it."

"Thanks." Marty sniffed twice suspiciously. "Any peanuts left?" she asked while neatly rearranging things on her side of the closet.

"Sure," Jeanne replied sheepishly and uncovered the buried treasure. "I skipped dessert," she remarked, feeling that an explanation was needed, "and tomorrow I'm going to start on my exercises again."

"Then why are you eating peanuts tonight?"

"Need the energy to study."

Marty opened her mouth and then thought better of it. There was no point in senseless arguing. With a preciseness that characterized all of her movements, she opened several books and arranged them in a semicircle on her desk. Removing her portable typewriter from its case, she positioned it in the middle of the books and placed some annotated cards at its side. "Going to try something," she said with resolution, "I'm going to try typing my paper for English directly from the books and notes without doing a first draft." She inserted two sheets with a carbon, then hesitated for the purpose of gathering her thoughts.

"Mine's finished," remarked Jeanne.

Marty looked up, much surprised. "Really?"

"Typed it before supper." She reached under the bed and withdrew a manila folder. "Here. Take a look if you don't believe me."

"I believe you all right," said Marty, getting out of her chair to accept the offered folder, "but you'll have to admit your assignments aren't usually finished ahead of time."

"This was sort of fun," Jeanne grinned, enjoying the attention.

Marty leafed through the pages, stopping occasionally to read a paragraph or section. Then she looked up from the essay and studied her roommate's round face still resting upon the pillow.

"What's the matter?" Jeanne asked, sitting up.

"Nothing—it's very good." Her voice reflected astonishment in discovering something academic that Jeanne could do well—very well, in fact. *People are always surprising you,* she thought cynically. *Inept Jeanne can write a well-coordinated paper on Faulkner, and Joyce with limitless talents can't hold together a marriage with Al Stoddard.* Marty had vowed to forget about the letter she had received from her mother that morning, at least until the tests were over. But her thoughts returned again and again to the stunning news that Al had pulled out, and that Joyce and Danny were now living at home, and had been for almost a month. That was the part that irritated Marty. No one had told her.

Jeanne watched and intuitively sensed that Marty was no longer thinking about the English paper. She scooted off the bed and slowly approached the darker-haired girl who was gazing blankly at the sheets in her hand.

"Do you need some typing paper?" Jeanne asked hesitantly.

"No," Marty replied, abruptly returning to reality. "In fact, I think I'll take my clutter downstairs and type in the kitchen."

"You won't bother me if you type in the room."

"I can think better alone anyway, and Mrs. Dickenson ought to be through in there by now." Marty closed the books, repacked the typewriter, and gathered up the cards and notes. She was acting even more strangely than usual in Jeanne's opinion, but the solidly established wall between them revealed no cracks or openings for further conversation. *She probably wants to talk to someone as much as I wish she would talk to me.* Jeanne allowed this thought to console her as Marty disappeared into the hallway, and the door closed behind her.

* * *

"All scripture is given by inspiration of God, and is profitable for—for—" Marty glanced down at the card propped up in front of her, "for doctrine, for reproof, for instruction in righteousness." She looked down again and corrected herself aloud, "Doctrine, reproof, *correction,* instruction in righteousness." After repeating it twice, she laid the card atop the others and decided to call it a night. Actually it had been morning for two and a half hours, but she was pleased to have finished her paper for English, done all the collateral reading for humanities, and memorized the required seven verses for the exam in Bible doctrine. The eager beavers who had hoarded the chairs in the lounge earlier in the evening had long since given up and crawled off to bed, and Marty silently padded around the kitch-en-lounge area in her slippered feet, enjoying a rare moment of privacy. The comfort of these minutes reminded her of another source of minor satisfaction which she had devised during these first months at Coastal. She stood quietly in the hallway, listen-ing for any sound to indicate that others were still awake. The dorm was silent, so Marty tiptoed into the darkened laundry room. Her practiced hand felt its way to the far end of the shelf containing detergent and other supplies and at last rested upon a small paper bag. She slipped the contents into the pocket of her robe, moved across the room, noiselessly opened the back door and then propped it open.

Marty shivered from the chilling November air as she sat down on the concrete slab that served as a back step to Cullen Hall. These nocturnal escapes from the dormitory's confining perimeter would soon be concluded with the approach of winter. Not that it made much difference, she admitted while taking the package of cigarettes out of her pocket. Smoking was no big deal. She'd gone along in high school when the situation seemed to require it, but it was no special hang-up. She wouldn't have bothered with the whole idea now, except that tobacco ranked so high on Coastal's list of absolute "no-noes." That alone made it extremely satisfying.

She struck a match, inhaled, and gently blew smoke in the direction of Mrs. Dickenson's window. Marty chuckled at her own daring, which remained within safe limits considering that only the housemother's kitchen window faced on this side of the building. She felt like blowing smoke toward Dr. Todd's and Miss Hawley's windows too, but not knowing where they lived made it somewhat difficult. The minutes passed peacefully with Marty finally crushing the cigarette on the side of the step and tossing the butt into a nearby hedge. Sometime next spring, when the gardening crew began trimming the brush around the dorm, they'd discover all this evidence she'd deposited. It would probably set off a scandal to rock the pure white foundations of good old Coastal. What a shame she'd be down at State and miss all the fun. Marty had trouble containing her giggle. She was getting tired and silly and perhaps even ready to go to bed. "Just a few more months," she murmured, letting herself back inside and returning her badge of independence to the brown paper bag.

* * *

The typewritten notice tacked to the bulletin board in Cullen's front hall read simply: "Urgent dorm council meeting. Attendance mandatory. 7 P.M. sharp."

"Wonder what's eating Annette now that she's called a midweek meeting?" Marty commented after reading the announcement.

"Who knows?" shrugged Sally Hoving who was standing behind her.

"Maybe she blew a test today, and we're supposed to pray that the prof won't notice the mistakes."

"Maybe," laughed Sally as she went upstairs.

Shortly before the seven o'clock hour Jeanne and Marty joined the girls already gathered in the lounge. An uncomfortable quiet hung over the room, possibly in deference to Miss Hawley who was sitting in a straight-backed chair near the fireplace. The presence of the dean of women, although unusual in itself, did not explain why most of the girls sat in silence, heads and eyes lowered. Jeanne viewed the scene with an uncertain sense of apprehension. *An accident?* she wondered. Something was wrong, and she too bowed her head to commit whatever it might be to the Lord.

"Is everyone here now?" Annette Perkins had assumed her place behind the small pine table. Her expression was sober.

"Sharon Bates was washing her hair; she'll be here in a minute," someone answered from the back.

Annette waited quietly until the delinquent Sharon, head covered with a towel, found a chair. "Mrs. Dickenson, would you open the meeting with prayer?" she requested.

The housemother rose. "Our Father," she prayed, and her voice imparted a tone of weariness, "grant us wisdom to deal with all matters as Thou would have us to, and make each of us aware of Thy presence in our daily lives. Amen."

That was quick, thought Marty, who had been timing prayer performances in chapel. By her unofficial records, Reverend Carding of the Bible department was the current champ.

"I will turn the remainder of the meeting over to Miss Hawley," said Annette in a move which surprised both Jeanne and Marty.

The reed-thin dean of women walked with determined strides to the speaker's table. Though she was no more slender nor less curvaceous than many fashion models, in her case the resulting impression was that of a mass of elbows and knees wired together by metal tubing. Her washed-out brown hair and pale blue eyes, hidden behind plastic-rimmed glasses, did nothing to distinguish her appearance. Ruth B. Hawley had assumed her present position at Coastal three years ago. Her predecessor had married a widowed pastor with five children, but Miss Hawley had not as yet found any marital candidates in connection with her work at the college, and each year that she moved farther into the shady side of thirty seemed to dim her prospects. It was suspected by faculty and students alike that Miss Hawley was on her way to becoming a campus tradition.

"Girls, it is with deep regret that I must speak to you this evening." The high-pitched voice strained to reach the back rows. "A serious matter has been brought to my attention, and I want this situation clarified before it becomes a more difficult problem. This morning, while Mrs. Dickenson was straightening up the clutter that some of you had left in the laundry room, she discovered a paper bag containing a partial package of cigarettes." Miss Hawley paused to allow the shock to settle in the minds of her listeners. "I consider this quite serious. The student or students who have been smoking are in direct violation of the school code and regulations. May I remind you that the

Lord already knows the guilty party, and she needs first to make this right with Him. In a Christian school, however, I think it is only fair to give an opportunity for the individual to stand and confess this sin to her dorm mates."

There was absolute silence. Jeanne glanced around to see whether anyone was going to stand.

"Girls, I'm waiting. First John 1:9 says that 'if we confess our sins, he is faithful and just to forgive us our sins, and to cleanse us from all unrighteousness.' I am not seeking to punish anyone—I want to help you if possible."

The room remained quiet. Jeanne looked over at Marty and was disappointed by the smirk on her roommate's face. It was just like Marty to think something like this was funny.

Miss Hawley took a deep breath. "All right, girls, I see no alternative but to ask that any of you knowing anything about this matter report the information to me. It is very likely that someone has noticed or observed something, and I feel that as Christians you have an obligation to make the truth known. I will be in Mrs. Dickenson's apartment for the next half hour and available to talk with any of you. Now I'm going to ask you to go to your rooms without congregating in the halls to discuss the situation, and I trust that you will be praying even as Mrs. Dickenson and I will be."

The lounge emptied quickly, and the girls filed down the hall and up the stairs without the usual jostling and giggling. Jeanne followed Marty into the room and shut the door behind her.

"Big deal!" said Marty, flopping down on the bed.

"Marty, this is serious. Things might go pretty rough when they find out who it was."

"How are they going to find out—check everyone's teeth for tobacco stains? Besides, how does old Hawley know that it wasn't a repairman or somebody that left the cancer sticks on the shelf? Oh, yeah, another thing—how come Mrs. D. is snooping around the stuff that belongs to the students? What happened to personal property rights?" Marty's voice was traced with belligerence.

Jeanne couldn't come up with any ready answers to that barrage. She walked over to the closet to get her robe, then stopped and turned around. "How did you know they found the bag on the shelf?"

"Where else would it have been?" She watched Jeanne's puzzled expression at these words. "What's the matter, roommate, are you getting suspicious? Maybe you'd better turn me in to the secret police downstairs because I know too much!"

Jeanne shook her head sadly. "You can smart off if you like, but I'm going to change my clothes, and then I'm going to pray about it like Miss Hawley suggested."

Marty's eyes sparkled, and an impish grin crossed her face. She opened her mouth to speak, thought better of it, then recklessly plowed in. "Yeah, I think you'd better pray."

"What's that supposed to mean?"

"Oh, nothing, except when I wore your robe last night I thought it smelled a little bit of tobacco."

"That's stupid," Jeanne replied indignantly and took the garment in question off the hanger. "It most certainly does not!"

"You haven't even smelled it yet." Marty laughed. "Go ahead. Sniff it all over—pockets especially."

Jeanne appeared confused, but then held the robe up to her nose.

"That's the way," Marty coached.

"Marty Miller, you're really not a bit funny, and I can't figure out why—" She suddenly stopped inspecting the robe and looked up with a bewildered stare. "It *does* smell like cigarettes —right here around the pocket."

"I thought you'd notice it too," Marty replied without cracking a smile.

"But—but—" Jeanne sputtered, and Marty couldn't keep back the laughter.

The other girl reddened. "Wait a minute. If that's what it is, it's because *you* wore it last night!"

Marty nodded. "OK, then you'd better take your story and your robe down to Hawley and Dickenson and see if they believe you. Then you can find out whether I'll admit to ever having worn that robe!"

The frown on Jeanne's broad face expanded. She shook her head slowly and sat down. "I don't want to tell anybody anything," she protested, "but I think you—"

"Oh, no," Marty interrupted, "not me! I'm not marching down to the confessional, because I don't care anything about Miss Hawley or what she said or about this crummy school either. But I figured you'd want to run right down there with what you know, so they'd pat you on the head and put three stars on your chart. Go on!" she taunted. "Just don't expect me to hang my head in guilt. I don't see how they can possibly prove a thing."

To Marty's annoyance, there was no response from her roommate. Jeanne remained in the chair, quietly concentrating on the floor and still frowning. The alarm clock on the dresser dominated the room with its rhythmic beat.

"Go on, Jeanne! You know you will sooner or later." Marty's hostility began to spill over, "Don't waste time thinking—just go follow the rules!"

"I'm not going anywhere."

"You didn't hear what Miss Hawley said about anyone who had any information?"

"I heard."

"Well, I'm telling you that I was out on the back steps smoking last night."

"OK."

"Man, I don't know what's gotten into you!" Marty's voice evidenced her growing frustration. "I thought 'Miss Perfect Christian Roommate' would love to have the opportunity of spreading around some truth and revelation. Maybe I'm a bad influence on you, huh? Next thing you know you'll skip prayer meeting or something. And then it'll be an easy step to—"

"Oh, Marty, stop it!" The tense lines in Jeanne's face began to twitch, and she hastily moved from the chair to the bed and buried her face in the sanctuary of her pillow.

Marty watched the sobbing figure with dismay. The perverse fun of the preceding minutes was gone; random thoughts and the remnants of her conscience tossed painfully inside. "Hey, I'm sorry," she finally stammered sheepishly. "I don't know what makes me so ornery sometimes, but I shouldn't have taken it out on you."

"It doesn't matter," was the muffled reply.

Marty turned toward the window, knowing somehow that it did matter. The words she had spoken seemed to hang in the air, and she didn't like having to stand back and listen to them. There were times, and this was one, when she hated what she saw in herself, but these feelings always passed—eventually. Often, however, they left a clinging and intangible residue which she found distinctly uncomfortable.

"Would you feel better if I tell Miss Hawley what I did? That'd get you off the hook for knowing, and I'm really not scared they'll do much to me, especially if I act like I'm sorry."

Jeanne wiped her eyes with the back of her hand and looked up.

"Well?" said Marty. She waited for a reply, but her roommate only shrugged in a hopeless and weary gesture. "Don't just lie there and look at me! I said I was sorry, and I'm trying to make things right."

Jeanne put her head back down on the pillow and closed her eyes.

"I guess I'm not very good at making things right," Marty commented softly and walked over to the door. "I'll be back after a while."

It seemed a long walk to the top of the staircase; she steadied herself on the bannister and descended. They could make her leave school, she supposed, but except for the loss of credits it wouldn't be any great tragedy. She didn't belong at Coastal anyway, though right at the moment it would be hard to say just where she did belong. Marty was suddenly uncertain and confused. She hesitated in front of Mrs. Dickenson's door, then knocked.

"Who is it?"

"Martha Miller."

"Come in, Martha."

"Is—is Miss Hawley still here?"

"No, she just left. Can I help you?"

Marty's composure was evaporating. She stood impassively before the housemother.

"Why don't you come on in," said Mrs. Dickenson, sensing something was wrong.

Marty obeyed woodenly and accepted the suggestion that she sit on the sofa.

"Would you like a cup of tea? I was just going to fix one for myself."

"Mrs. Dickenson," she said mechanically, "those were my cigarettes you found. I know I broke the rules, and I'll take whatever the punishment is."

The housemother walked back from the doorway and took a seat opposite Marty. "Well, of course this is a matter for Miss Hawley to consider, but she is quite understanding, and I'm sure she'll appreciate your honesty. Uh—is smoking a special problem for you, Martha?"

Marty had an impulse to laugh at the irony and innocence of this question, but she was momentarily very tired. The assault her conscience had launched was becoming burdensome, and she wanted to run. The direction didn't matter just as long as there was a crowd and some noise, and she didn't have to think. "It's no special problem," she said, getting up.

"Then what is it?"

"I don't know," replied Marty with haste. The feeling of entrapment, both in this room and in her thoughts, was growing more intense. "It's just me, I guess." She started for the door. "I'll talk to Miss Hawley in the morning, or you can call and tell her tonight; it doesn't matter."

"What is it that you think is wrong with you?" Mrs. Dickenson persisted.

This time Marty did laugh, a little bitterly. "Oh, there are all kinds of things wrong with me," she answered, trying to toss it off lightly. "I break rules just for the heck of it. I torment people into tears just for the heck of it. I—I—" The words wouldn't come out, and she was afraid that she was about to make a fool out of herself. Her hand was on the doorknob.

"And are you happy?"

Marty stood motionless while her mind wavered. At last she loosened her grip on the doorknob and slowly returned to her place on the sofa. "No," she said quietly, "I'm not. I've never felt more miserable in my whole life than I do right now."

"Perhaps God has been giving you a good look at yourself for a purpose."

The girl nodded as unwanted tears formed in her eyes.

"We have to see things as they really are in order to understand how completely separated we are from God. But there is a way for man to be at peace with his Creator, you know."

Marty's expression was dubious. She sighed deeply, then shook her head. "It's just not all that simple."

"It's exactly that simple—if it's what you want."

The silence which followed supported the growing tension in the room. Marty's breathing was audible, but her eyes remained riveted on the floor. Her left hand nervously clenched and unclenched an imaginary object, and at last she covered her forehead with the other. "I guess I do want it," she said softly, "but I've been fighting this so long—I don't even know how to begin."

"Just tell God you want Christ's death to cover your own sins."

"I can't," Marty replied, shaking her head again. "I—I can't."

"Now—tell Him now, Martha, while your heart is ready."

She swallowed and tried to speak. "Dear God," she began, and then her voice broke. "Please help me," Marty sobbed.

Mrs. Dickenson moved over to the sofa and put her arms around the distraught girl. "Tell Him," she quietly encouraged.

"I'm—I'm sorry for all of it," Marty prayed brokenly, "and for hating everybody, and I know I need Christ, and—O, God, help me—" She buried her face in the housemother's ample shoulder.

"It's all right now, Martha." Mrs. Dickenson soothed and wiped tears from her own eyes. "Everything's going to be all right."

* * *

After the excitement and elation of the preceding evening, Jeanne found it difficult to get up at 6:30 A.M. as she had planned, especially since Marty continued to sleep soundly, face turned toward the wall. Summoning all the reserves in her short supply of willpower, Jeanne managed to dress and stumble down the road to Harrison Hall by seven. Bacon and coffee aromas drifting from the dining area into the main hall succeeded in dispelling her drowsiness even though the brisk walk in the morning air had not. She looked around for Pete and saw that he had just passed the serving tables. With luck she could probably find a seat near him. She got into the cafeteria line behind the other early birds and mentally rehearsed how she was going to tell Pete about the answer to their prayers, at the same time collecting her tray, silverware, bacon and eggs, and two packages of cornflakes.

Pete Bradley was seated at a table by himself, more intent on reviewing his Greek vocabulary cards than on eating breakfast. He watched Jeanne approaching and with an inward sigh rose to help with her tray.

"Good morning," she greeted him brightly.

"Morning," he replied.

Jeanne arranged the food in front of her, then bowed her head to pray. Pete jumped at the opportunity to return to his vocabulary cards before all the inane small talk began.

"I have a lot to thank God for this morning," she commented after opening her eyes.

"Good," he muttered, still concentrating on the cards.

"Marty accepted the Lord last night."

This time Pete looked up, surprise and instantaneous joy evident in his smile. "Really?"

"She went down to see Mrs. Dickenson for about an hour last night, and when she came back she was a different person. You just can't believe the change!"

"Hey, that's great—that's really great!"

Jeanne beamed, terribly pleased at his reaction. "I knew you'd be thrilled as much as I was. It's so wonderful to be at a Christian school where we can know real prayer fellowship and the bond of sharing God's blessings."

"Does everyone know about this?" he continued, still thinking about Marty.

"Oh, no, I don't think so—I wanted to tell you first. Maybe she could give her testimony in prayer meeting tonight."

"That might be rushing things. I'd like to talk to her this morning. Does she have a class second hour?"

"Let's see, this is Wednesday. No, she's free then."

"Real good."

"I'm just so happy I can hardly eat," Jeanne bubbled, and Pete watched with a smile as she added a third teaspoon of sugar to her coffee.

* * *

Pete was standing in the hallway when Marty emerged from her first-hour English class. "Have you got a few minutes to talk?" he asked.

"Sure," she smiled in return. The hard lines around her mouth and the determined set of her eyes had been replaced by a softness and radiance, and Pete looked at her tenderly, thrilling again to the miracle of a new creation in Jesus Christ.

"Why don't you leave your books in the lounge, and we'll take a walk," he said, guiding her by the arm through the between-classes crowd.

They stopped in the lounge long enough to unburden the load of books, and long enough to attract the attention of everyone in the room. Then together they went out the side door and, with Pete leading the way, followed the narrow sidewalk around to the rear of the building. The sun had warmed the early morning chill, and the grass and shrubbery sparkled with moisture from the recent rain.

"Are you afraid of getting your shoes wet?" he asked, indicating a dirt path which encircled the supply buildings and led up the hill.

"They'll wash."

"Then let's go up to the Lookout."

Marty followed the path as directed, breathing in the fragrance of the dampened brush and savoring life itself. "Would you believe that I've never been up to the Lookout before?" she asked innocently.

Pete laughed, "Little girl, you've got a lot to learn about college life at Coastal."

"I've heard a few reports," she replied.

They walked for about a quarter of a mile along the sloping hillside trail until reaching a shaded point that jutted out and afforded a panoramic view of the campus and surrounding farmland. In years past enterprising male students had taken logs up the trail and under this clump of trees and brush constructed two roughhewn benches. A six-inch-wide stripe had been painted across the center of both benches as a reminder of Coastal's unwritten law governing "conduct between members of the opposite sex."

"This is it," said Pete.

Marty smiled and sat down. "I like it," she said simply.

He leaned against the bank, broke off a twig and shredded it into small pieces. "You probably think I'm crazy to bring you clear up here just to talk, but it seemed like too fine a morning not to get outside somewhere." He hesitated momentarily. "Jeanne told me that you found the Lord last night. I'm real happy for you, Marty."

"I'm happy too," she said thoughtfully, "happier than I ever dreamed was possible. I wish I hadn't been so stupid and stubborn and had done it a lot sooner."

"God's ways in God's time."

"Yes," she agreed and looked out over the college grounds.

"Coastal looks somewhat different to you today, huh?"

She blushed slightly. "I've been a real stinker—counting off the days until I could get away from here and everything. Now I just hope that God will let me stay at Coastal. There's so much for me to learn and so many things to make right."

"Do you still feel the same way about the school's social events?"

"What?" she asked, not understanding.

"I was wondering if you'd go to the sophomore banquet with me?"

"You don't have to do that," she said, embarrassed by what she felt to be a good-will gesture on his part.

"I know I don't have to." Pete grinned. "In fact, I haven't asked anyone for the past two years."

"But you're just doing it because of what has happened, and that's really not necessary."

"I'm asking you because I want to, and I'm not going to commit myself any further. Will you go with me?"

"I'd love to."

They stayed at the Lookout for another fifteen minutes, sometimes joking, sometimes talking seriously; and Pete prayed aloud before starting back for the next class. They trudged down the winding path, each engrossed in his own thoughts—Marty, anxious to find Jeanne and share this latest "good news," and

Pete, wondering where he would scrape up the extra cash for two banquet tickets.

From Classroom 212 located on the back corner of Harrison's second floor Jeanne watched Pete and Marty return to the main campus. Mr. Lawrence's lecture had begun to ramble in the last few minutes, and she had been concentrating on the two figures on the hillside which was clearly visible from the nearby window. Her heart had skipped a beat when she recognized them; how perfectly things were working out for these important people in her college life. She was confident that living with Marty would be much easier now, and the prayer victory which she and Pete had shared might be the basis for a deeper friendship, and —Jeanne smiled, knowing she shouldn't get her hopes too high. *But after all,* she thought, *nothing is impossible with God.*

4

Al

"AL, WILL YOU CLEAR OUT the registers and cover the center-aisle tables? I've got to go up to Personnel and see about getting some extras for tomorrow."

"Yeah, sure, OK, aye, aye, sir," Al Stoddard muttered under his breath as Mr. Fredrickson headed for the escalator.

"Oh, and Al, be in by 8:30 in the morning," he called back. "Carl and I have to be at a division managers' meeting, and you'll have to set out those items for the 99¢ table by yourself."

Al nodded his acknowledgment and glared sullenly after the rotund figure of his boss as it disappeared from view. He was tired of being stuck with all the dirty work in the department. Mr. Fredrickson was exempt from doing anything other than giving orders, it seemed, and Carl Denton was enjoying all the rights and privileges that seemed to come with a promotion. Carl was a good guy, but it was hard not to resent someone coming into the department in September and being made number-two man right away.

Finishing with the registers, Al dug out the white covers from under the counter and began throwing them over the tables. The 5:40 bell rang, Sealy Brothers' signal that employees were now free to punch the time clock; more accurately, that they had better punch the time clock before the second bell rang, and Al started for the cashier's window with the day's receipts. The general kidding and talking among those waiting to get their

79

timecards out of the rack irritated him this evening, and he pushed in front of two ladies from Infants' Wear in order to get away from the place sooner.

Outside, the glare from the multicolored lights which formed an archway for six blocks on Gower Street reminded him that beginning tomorrow the store would be staying open every evening until Christmas. He had intended to say something to Mr. Fredrickson this afternoon about working out a schedule so that he could still play ball, but after bungling a six-carbon easy-payment plan and dock pick up it hadn't seemed the right time to mention it. Al stuck his hands in his jacket pocket and made his way through the crowd of late afternoon shoppers. The car was parked in the corner lot and, after redeeming his ticket, he pulled out into the traffic. He considered the possibility of going to Barney's Grill for a steak and a couple of beers, but decided against it. He was short on money already this week, and then Bud had been on his back for drinking before games. Cruising through the main part of town and trying to think of some alternative to the Burger Basket, on a sudden impulse he pulled in at a service station with a pay phone out in front. Al searched his pockets for a dime and a crumpled slip of paper, then ambled over to the booth. He dialed the number and fidgeted while waiting for an answer.

"Hello."

"Pam?"

"Yes."

"Pam, this is Al—Al Stoddard."

"Al?" Her voice was uncertain and questioning.

"I've missed seeing you at our games," he said with his old confidence in these situations returning.

"Well, since Bud and I broke things off, I've kind of stayed away from places where I know he'll be."

"Uh—would it be all right if I dropped by to see you for a few minutes?"

"You and Joyce?"

"No, I'm by myself. Haven't you heard that Joyce and I are all through?"

"Somebody said something, but I didn't know whether to believe it or not."

"Yeah, it's true." He hesitated, "Is it OK if I come by?"

"Well, Al, I'm real sorry but I've already made plans to go out in a little bit and—"

"OK," he said, catching a change of inflection in her voice. "See you around, Pam."

He placed the receiver back on the hook and listlessly returned to the parked car. His appetite was spoiled, but out of habit he drove by the Burger Basket and picked up two hamburgers and an order of fries "to go." With a sack of food on the front seat beside him, he headed the car out to the darkened high school gym, where he parked and waited out the hour and a half till gametime.

* * *

A thin mist of hair spray hung over the room as Marty stepped back from the mirror to inspect the finished effect. The pale green woolen sheath accented the color of her eyes, and she smiled in self-satisfaction.

"It's really lovely," said Jeanne wistfully.

Marty turned to her roommate who was lounging on the bed with a candy bar and a novel. "Does my slip show any in the back?"

"Nope, you look great."

"I wish you'd change your mind and go with us," remarked Marty as she got her coat from the closet. "It doesn't seem fair for you to stay home after you spent all that time helping to wrap the presents."

"Those kids at the hospital won't miss my shining face a bit, and I had fun with the wrapping anyhow."

"You really won't come along? Pete said to be sure to ask you."

"Three's a crowd," stated Jeanne flatly.

"Don't be silly; we want you to come."

"Marty," said Jeanne with a little edge to her voice, "you don't know what it's like to drag along on somebody else's date because you've never had to do it. I have. My older sister and her boyfriend used to take me to things when I was in high school and, believe me, I'll stay home any night rather than go through that again. Besides, this book is just getting good, and I'll be all through with it before you get home."

"What are you reading?" Marty asked, deciding not to pursue her point about the Christmas party at Children's Hospital any further.

Jeanne flipped the book over to look at the cover. *High upon a Rock,* she read. "I found it in the library."

"Why do you read that junky fiction stuff?"

"Because I like it."

"Good enough reason," Marty commented amiably as she walked to the window and peeked through the curtain. There were a few cars parked in front of the dorm, although most of the students had already left for Harwood.

"Pete's late tonight," observed Jeanne.

"He's got that extra job gardening at the Grayson place down the road on Tuesdays and Thursdays, so he was going to have to shower and change before picking me up. You know, Jeanne, it makes me feel like a crumb for him to be taking me out and spending money on dates when he needs it so badly to pay school expenses."

"He wouldn't do it if he didn't want to."

Marty smiled again, her heart full and overflowing with the joys of these recent weeks. "He's pretty terrific," she said dreamily.

The buzzer from downstairs rang twice. "That must be Pete," exclaimed Marty, grabbing her coat. "See you later, Jeanne. Be good."

"Have fun," Jeanne called after her and with a heavy spirit turned back to her book.

Pete was waiting at the bottom of the stairs. "Sorry it took so long," he greeted her.

"You might be worth waiting for," she teased as they went out the door.

"Jeanne didn't want to come?" he asked.

"No, she didn't want to break in on our date."

"That's too bad."

"Yes, it is," said Marty, perturbed at what had happened. "Do those guys that live in your dorm realize how much it would mean to some of the girls in Cullen just to have a date once in a while?"

Pete shrugged his shoulders. "Don't know. The guys have their problems too."

"Well, I wish you could find someone over there who would ask Jeanne out," Marty persisted.

"It was hard enough finding someone who would take you out!" he said, opening the car door.

"Pow!" She faked a right jab to his nose and laughingly got in.

* * *

Paul Herbert paused at the corner to ascertain whether his aching knee would allow him a choice of routes home. After some hesitation he decided upon the longer of the two, hoping to stimulate his thinking by the added exercise. It had been a very disturbing day—and so totally unexpected. He shifted the sack containing milk and a loaf of bread to his other arm and shuffled along the darkened street. Yes, it had really come unexpectedly, though perhaps he had merely failed to notice the signs of discontent. His first-year German class had complained earlier in the semester about the delay in getting their exams back, but it had only been four days this time, and the scores had been generally good. Even Bobby Jordan had improved over his mark on the midterm, though he continued to hold his position at the bottom of the class curve. The grade sheet had been posted outside the German department office shortly before class, and by the time Dr. Herbert walked into the room his desk was encircled by a group of irate basketball players. The professor shook his head sadly as he crossed the street and began the last block home. Never before had students walked out on one of his classes, nor had there ever been complaints to higher authorities about his teaching skills. Nevertheless, he was not going to give Jordan a provisionally passing mark when he didn't deserve it—basketball team or no basketball team. Paul Herbert emphasized this point firmly with a gesture to some unseen audience and turned up his own front walk. He would fix some cocoa for Frieda, and then they would just go to bed and forget the whole matter.

The old man turned the key in the lock, pushing the door open with his shoulder. Immediately he was overwhelmed by the smell of gas. Rushing directly to the kitchen, he found gas escaping from all the jets on the stove. He snapped the burners off and threw open the windows. He ran on, as though playing an impeded role in a nightmare, searching desperately for Frieda. She was lying on the floor in the bedroom and, with his remaining strength, Dr. Herbert pulled and dragged her through the front room and out onto the lawn.

"Help me!" he gasped. "Somebody help!"

He was himself breathing with difficulty, and it seemed an eternity before porch lights flickered and front doors opened at two neighboring houses.

"What's the matter out there?"

"It's my wife," Dr. Herbert called. "Somebody, help me!"

In moments the street was filled with anxious and sympathetic onlookers, and the elderly professor was crowded aside as others gathered around Frieda's still body lying on the grass.

"Call an ambulance!" someone directed.

"Try mouth-to-mouth resuscitation," another voice suggested.

Dr. Herbert stood back. It was like watching a program on TV—dramatic, frightening, yet completely unrelated to himself. His thoughts were confused, and he suddenly realized that he had not even prayed. Sitting down on the grass away from the activity, he covered his eyes with his hand and for the moment rested in the presence of his God. No particular words or phrases came to mind, nor were they needed to assure perfect communion.

"Is he all right?" Two figures were at his side, helping him to his feet. Their faces were indistinguishable and shapeless, and the professor wondered briefly what all the commotion was about. He stared vacantly at the ambulance parked at the curb.

"He took a lot of gas too," a man explained to a white-coated attendant.

The attendant nodded and took Dr. Herbert by the arm. "Let's climb in back, fella. Your wife's going to be all right. Don't worry about a thing."

He did as directed, the door closing immediately behind him. With siren blaring, the vehicle pulled away from the little house. Frieda was lying on the stretcher. In spite of his dizziness he moved over to where he could hold her hand. She smiled at his touch and murmured something about having Christmas dinner on the table before one o'clock. He pressed her hand to his cheek and wept unashamedly.

* * *

The lump in Marty's throat persisted long after they had left the ward. She was discovering that the presence of Jesus Christ in her life opened her eyes to many things she previously had not noticed. This had been true all evening at the party Coastal had sponsored at Children's Hospital. Her heart had been touched by several of these little ones, and the desire to actively do something for them had inundated her being.

"It's hard to shake off an evening like that, isn't it?" Pete remarked as they walked slowly toward the main parking lot.

She appreciated his instinctive understanding of her mood. "I—I just can't put it into words. Things are so perfect for me right now—so absolutely perfect. You know how completely happy I am. And then to see those little kids and all their problems— Well, I—I just want to share some of all that I have with them. I'm not making much sense, am I?"

"You're making perfect sense. That's part of the Holy Spirit's ministry in our lives, to make us sensitive and aware of the needs of others. But the physical needs are not really the most important part, Marty."

"I understand that," she said as he held the car door open for her, "but being able to visualize a need seems to make it that much more real to me."

He got in beside her and turned the key in the ignition. "I'm glad to know you've got a soft heart under all that polish," he said, smiling as he backed the car out into the lot and then headed toward the exit. Checking the traffic, he made a right turn onto the street. "Hungry?" he asked.

"Not particularly," she replied. "About that soft-heart bit, you've hit on a painful truth."

"You try to keep it covered up, huh?"

"Have to," she grinned, "or I'd be mopping tears all day long."

"The Lord can use that kind of a heart. Have you ever thought much about missions?"

"Not especially. I'm not anxious to get involved with bugs and snakes and, as far as that goes, most of the missionaries I've seen haven't been too impressive—you know, high collars and no makeup and all that."

Pete didn't pursue the subject further. He guided the car out of the city streets of Harwood and onto the highway. The cool night air whistled through a permanent crack in the rear window, and Marty was bothered by the sudden silence.

"I had a letter from my sister today," she began.

"Are things going any better with her husband?"

"It doesn't sound like it. She said he's really gone off the deep end lately, and nobody's been able to talk to him. I guess he's drinking a lot."

"She and the baby are still there with your folks?"

Marty nodded. "It's going to seem funny going home for vacation next week and having them in the house. Joyce sounds miserable by her letters. I'd like to talk to Al while I'm home and tell him about the difference in my own life, but he probably wouldn't listen. I wish you could talk to him, Pete."

He shrugged his shoulders. "I couldn't say anything that someone else probably hasn't already said."

"When are you leaving for home?" Marty asked, an idea popping into her thought processes.

"I'm not. The Graysons are going to be gone over the holidays, and they've hired me to baby-sit with their garden and their dogs."

"You're going to stay up here all by yourself?" asked Marty incredulously.

"I did it last year."

"You spent Christmas day all alone?"

"No, Dr. and Mrs. Todd had me over for dinner."

"Well, if you're going to be stuck here this year, why don't you drive down to Santa Alberta and have Christmas with us? My folks would love to have you, and maybe you might even get a chance to talk with Al. Really, I'm serious about this."

"Well, thanks for the invitation. We'll see what works out," he said lightly.

"If nothing better comes along, huh?" Marty teased, wanting to get away from the serious atmosphere before the elusive Mr. Bradley sensed some sort of trap.

"Mr. Grayson's mother is a widow and a big success in the stock market. I've been sort of looking for an angle there. Of course, she's eighty-five, so I may have to hurry!"

"I knew that job must have fringe benefits," she laughed.

"Just making the most of my opportunities." Pete grinned and stepped on the accelerator taxing the little Falcon to the limit of its endurance.

* * *

A flurry of activities preceded the Christmas vacation for

Coastal Bible College students. Professors redeemed the time
by working in a few extra quizzes; dorm students arranged several impromptu late-evening parties. On the afternoon of December 19th the large-scale campus exodus began. Jeanne Robbins boarded a bus in the Harwood station, her suitcases loaded
with textbooks and her mind mulling over the various experiences she would have to share with her family. Pete Bradley,
who was running a shuttle service between campus and the
station with the old wagon, waved good-bye and felt a spark of
envy for those whose families were expecting them home for
Christmas. Not that his folks wouldn't like it too, but the money he would earn during the holidays would cover the rest of
what he owed on his first semester's bill. Second semester? He
pushed the thought from his mind, knowing that the Lord
couldn't expect him to solve this problem by himself.

Marty Miller had a ride home with Fred Korinsky who was
driving through to San Diego. The idea of relaxing and doing
nothing appealed tremendously, although she too had packed
some books and intended to finish her term paper for English.
She also brought the small devotional book that Pete had
given her shortly before they had said good-bye on the front
lawn of Harrison. He had said "Merry Christmas," although
the book had not been wrapped, and she had been disappointed
to find nothing written inside the cover. Hopefully these two
weeks away from school would also give her a chance to assess
what exactly was their relationship. She was uncertain of her
own feelings, and even more uncertain of his. Marty also anticipated seeing the old high school gang, possibly even hearing
from Richie—though he hadn't written since early in October.
She hoped he would call, just so she might tell him how wrong
she had been about the Bible school and about Christ and about
so much.

Marty had been home for three days before she got around to
telling her mother about her invitation to Pete for Christmas
day. Mrs. Miller was somewhat less than enthusiastic.

"You invited him for Christmas day," she asked, only slightly covering her exasperation. "Oh, Marty, won't that be rather difficult? I mean, Joyce thinks Al will at least come by and bring Danny something, and having a stranger here will make it—" Her voice trailed off uncertainly.

"But, Mom, he was going to be all by himself. I couldn't do anything but invite him."

"No, I suppose you couldn't."

"Besides, I hope he does get to meet Al. He might be just the person who could reach him. You guys just don't know how terrific Pete is."

"Sounds like you're convinced," said Joyce who had been listening to the conversation from the kitchen.

Marty blushed inadvertently. "We're just good friends."

"I've heard that one before," her sister laughed.

Marty smiled, knowing that she had heard it a few times before too, and wondering for the first time whether Jeanne's "friendship" with Pete had carried the same undertones as her own. *Probably not,* she decided. *Jeanne's so sincere and such a sold-out Christian that she'd probably never get tied up in her own emotions like I do.*

"Is it OK then if I call him tonight?" she asked, having given her mother time to consider the matter.

"It doesn't sound like there's much choice," her mother replied wearily.

"Don't worry about it, Mom," Joyce interjected. "Marty and I are going to take care of Christmas dinner for you, and we'll get things straightened up."

Marty gulped at the suggestion. "I don't know if I want to impress Pete with my cooking ability."

"He's just a friend, remember?" teased Joyce.

"He won't even be that by the time we get through with the meal, that is, unless you've improved an awful lot lately."

Joyce maintained her smile with effort, but her voice was serious. "I've been trying harder along those lines, sis."

"I'm sorry, Joyce. I didn't mean that to sound the way it did."

"That's OK. We've both learned a few lessons this year. Right?"

"Right," Marty agreed wholeheartedly.

That evening, while the rest of the family dozed in front of the blaring TV, Marty put in her long-distance call to Harwood. She cleared her throat several times as it rang, and licked her lips.

"Grayson residence, Peter Bradley speaking."

"You sound just like the butler in those horror movies," Marty giggled, forgetting her nervousness.

"Well, hello there, little freshman. How's it going?"

"Real fine. How are you?"

"Tired," he admitted. "I just got in."

"Big date?"

"Yeah—Doc and Mrs. Herbert."

"Oh, how's she getting along?"

"She's going strong as ever now, but this thing has really set Doc back. I'm kind of worried about him; he doesn't feel he can leave her alone anymore, even for a few minutes."

"That's too bad," Marty sympathized. "Uh—what I called you about was to see if you will be able to come down for Christmas."

"Well—" he hesitated.

"I've talked to Mom, and it's fine with her."

"Well, if you're sure I won't be in the way."

"Not at all," Marty said, happy that her beaming face was not visible across the telephone lines. "When can you be here?"

"I can be at your place by noon on the 25th and wouldn't have to be back here until the morning of the 27th, if that's OK with your folks."

"It's terrific," she enthused. "I'll have time to give you the complete scenic tour of the area."

"I might get worried if you know too many secluded scenic spots," he kidded.

Marty laughed, unable to think of a good comeback. "I better cut this off before I run up Daddy's phone bill. We'll see you in a couple of days then."

"I'm looking forward to it. Good night, Marty."

"Good night," she replied softly and placed the receiver down. Her heart was doing flips. "Oh, thank You, Lord," she whispered and sailed off for the privacy of her own room.

* * *

Joyce and Marty kept their pledge and, with a domestic enthusiasm rare in both of them, the house was polished and decorated, and an elaborate holiday dinner was prepared. By noon Danny and his grandpa had retired into a corner to assemble a miniature train and track, and Mrs. Miller had disappeared into the kitchen to make a final check on the turkey. The girls sat together on the sofa, much as they would have years earlier. Marty had been keeping one eye on the clock all morning and now watched the front window with growing restlessness. Joyce, wearied by the pretense of joy which she had been carefully displaying, viewed her younger sister and, in spite of good intentions, was envious and somewhat impatient.

"It's only ten after twelve," she stated flatly.

Marty quickly looked away from the window, embarrassed to have been caught. She smiled sheepishly.

"You're really serious about this guy, aren't you?" asked Joyce, amazed at the reaction her chance remark had caused and aware for the first time that this was something different from Marty's previous crushes.

"You'll have to meet him to understand," replied Marty simply, "but don't expect any big romance. If there is one, he doesn't know about it yet."

Joyce laughed and shook her head. "There are times I have to remind myself that this is really you!"

"I have the same problem," Marty grinned.

"Never saw a finer looking turkey," commented Mrs. Miller, returning to the front room. "It ought to be done by one o'clock." She glanced over at Joyce, trying to measure her feelings before asking the question that had come to mind. "Should we set a place for Al?"

"I told him when we'd be eating when he called last night, but he didn't say whether he'd stay for dinner or not."

"Did you invite him?" her mother asked.

"Not exactly."

"I can't see Al passing up a good meal under any circumstances," Marty broke in, but was quickly silenced by her mother's cold glare.

"Well, I think I'll go ahead and set a place for him anyway," said Mrs. Miller. "Then if he does decide—" She stopped in the middle of the sentence. "Does your friend drive a white Falcon, Marty?"

Marty turned her head toward the window and stifled an excited squeal. "That's him!" she cried, taking off for her bedroom. "One of you let him in!"

Mrs. Miller looked at Joyce, who threw her hands in the air in a hopeless gesture. "I think you and Dad had better take a good look at Pete while he's here," she said with an amused tone. "Little sis seems pretty interested."

"At least things never get dull around this house," the older woman said half to herself as she crossed toward the front door. Her arrival coincided with the ring of the bell, and she hesitated a few seconds before opening the door.

"Mrs. Miller?"

The young man, slim-faced and blond, stood with suitcase beside him on the front steps. He was not particularly imposing in his build or manner of dress, and a twinge of motherly disappointment surged through her at her daughter's choice, if this he truly was. "Do come in, Pete, we've been expecting you," she said with automatic warmth.

"Hi! I thought maybe you'd chickened out," Marty greeted him, coming into the entry hall.

Pete's face relaxed and the normal smile appeared. "Not a chance."

"Why don't you leave your things here in the hall—we can take them to your room later," Mrs. Miller directed as she led him into the living room. Marty hurriedly followed and took over the responsibility for the introductions.

"Pete, this is my dad, and my sister, Joyce, and my nephew, Danny." Mr. Miller stiffly stood up from the newly erected railroad yard and shook hands with Pete. Joyce nodded and smiled while Danny ignored the interruption in typical two-year-old fashion. Marty felt self-conscious and ill at ease. It was not as though she had never brought a boy into the house before. Richie had camped in front of the TV many evenings, irritating her parents by his crude remarks and enormous appetite. But with Richie she had almost defied her family to like him, and at the moment she felt like pleading with them to accept Pete and appreciate him as she did.

"Well, did you have an easy trip down from the school?" her father began.

"Very easy, sir." Pete answered, taking the chair that had been offered him. "Not much traffic on Christmas morning."

"No, I suppose not."

Mrs. Miller cleared her throat. "It must be hard on your family to have you away from home on the holidays. Where is it that you're from? Marty has probably mentioned it, but I've forgotten."

"Clarington. It's a little town in eastern Washington. I've lived there all my life."

"What sort of business is your dad in, Pete?" Mr. Miller asked, searching to put the conversation into a familiar territory.

"He has a wheat farm."

"I don't suppose this has been too good a year for farmers, has it?"

"Not too good," agreed Pete ruefully.

"No, sir," Mr. Miller said, shaking his head sadly. "Why, I

was telling a fellow down at the office just the other day, if this administration gets us through another two years without a primary recession the voters ought to have enough sense to stay with a good thing. Do you realize what the opposition would do with the current economic situation if they were in power? Well, let me tell you, it would be a sorry day for all of us little fellows."

Marty shot a glance at Joyce who caught the cue and popped in another question while her father paused for breath. "You're a senior at Coastal, aren't you?" she asked.

"That's right."

"Do you know what you'll be doing after graduation?"

"I hope to go on to seminary next year."

"A preacher?" questioned Mrs. Miller politely.

"Well, more exactly, I think the Lord wants me on the mission field."

Marty's surprise at this last statement was equaled by that of her family whose first real acquaintance with missionaries had begun when they started attending Grace Church. Before that it had been limited to the pictures presented in popular fiction and on TV's late-late show. The group was suddenly quiet for several seconds until Mrs. Miller started back for the kitchen, mumbling something about the gravy.

"Why don't I show you where you'll be tonight and you can get washed up?" Marty suggested.

"Sounds like a good idea," he replied and followed her out into the hall. He picked up the suitcase and walked in silence as she led him to a room at the far end of the hallway.

"It's a little cluttered," she apologized. "Those are Joyce's things in the boxes; we don't have anyplace else to put them. But maybe you can find enough space to turn around in."

"It's fine." He looked at her with a slight bit of humor in his expression. "Relax, Marty, everything's fine as far as I'm concerned."

"It shows that much, huh?" she laughed softly. "I was just

afraid that Dad would tree you on the political issue. Then, of course, you kind of floored them by saying you were going to be a missionary. How come you never told me that?"

"You never asked me."

The natural ease between them had returned and Marty went over to sit down on the bed. "I guess I just assumed that you were planning on the ministry."

"I am," he said, sitting down beside her. "What difference does it make where I preach the gospel?"

"I suppose it doesn't really make any difference," Marty admitted.

"Only that I want to be in the exact place that the Lord has for me, and I'm very confident that He will lead me there as long as I am willing."

"I'm sure you're right; you usually are," she said, smiling. "Just remember, my folks are Christians, but they've never gone too far with it or studied very much. To them, missionaries are pretty odd ducks."

"And what are they to you?"

"I'm not really sure," was her troubled reply.

"Don't let it worry you," he said, getting up. "Man, it smells like turkey—I'm starved!"

She stood up and smoothed out the spread. "Dinner's all ready. We're just sort of waiting to see if Al will show up."

"Do you think he will?"

"He likes to eat."

"Well, that's something in his favor."

They rejoined the family in the living room, Pete taking time to inspect Danny's carefully guarded loot.

"Everything all right?" asked Mrs. Miller.

"Fine," Pete replied, "I really appreciate your inviting me down to share your Christmas."

"It's our pleasure. Do you think we should go ahead with dinner?" she asked, turning to Joyce.

"Might as well, I guess." Her disappointment was only thinly veiled as she walked over to the front window for one last hopeful look. "Wait!" she exclaimed with a comingling of surprise and relief. Then her face paled.

"Is it Al?" her mother asked anxiously.

"Yes," Joyce replied firmly. "Let me handle this alone."

Marty moved over to where she had a view of the street. Al's two-door hardtop was parked at the curb, and he was coming up the front walk. His attractive blonde companion had chosen to wait in the car. Marty put her hand on her sister's arm, but Joyce pulled away and started for the door.

"Be easy," Marty whispered. She turned to the others, suddenly feeling in a position of command and, with a nod of the head, indicated the direction of the kitchen. They disappeared around the corner just as Joyce opened the door and faced her husband for the first time in almost a month.

"Hello, Joyce," Al said quietly. "I brought this for Danny." He was carrying a large package covered with Sealy Brothers' traditional Christmas paper.

"Come in. He's in the living room."

Al wiped his feet on the mat and stepped inside.

"Daddy!" shrilled Danny who had been drawn to the sound of the voices. "Hi, Daddy!"

"Hello there, little man," said Al, picking him up.

"Mo' toy," the two-year-old announced, poking at the package in his father's arms. Al set him down and placed the gift in front of him. Schooled by the experience of the morning, Danny immediately tore into the paper and uncovered a large stuffed animal. "Cow!" he proclaimed loudly.

"Horsie," Al corrected.

"Cow, G'ampa, see cow!" He took the animal by the ear and dragged it off to the kitchen.

"Would you like to sit down?" said Joyce awkwardly.

"No, thanks. I—I have to be going." He hesitated for a moment, then his curiosity won out. "Whose car is that parked out front?"

"Pete Bradley's. He's a friend of Marty's from school."

"Oh. Well, Merry Christmas, Joyce." He backed toward the door, stepping over the wrapping paper under his feet.

"Thanks. Same to you," she replied coldly. "I appreciate you coming by to see Danny today."

"Yeah, it was good to see him. Good-bye, Joyce."

She closed the door behind him, took several deep breaths, and began to move slowly to the dining area off the den where the others had gathered. The good china and the silverware glistened on the white linen tablecloth, and the centerpiece of silver ornaments and red poinsettias reflected gaily in the candle-light, but all eyes were focused grimly on the empty place at Joyce's side.

* * *

It wasn't until evening that Marty had any opportunity to be alone with Pete. After they had finished the dishes that had been used for the late afternoon dessert, and her father had at last found an excuse to turn on the TV, Pete suggested that they go outside for some much needed exercise. The air was crisp, and the lighted trees on display in practically every window set a picture-book scene, at least in Marty's romantic imagination. Her dream world was made complete when he gently took her hand as they strolled along, talking lightly of school, friends and incidentals. Eventually the conversation centered on Al and Joyce.

"I wouldn't mind having a chance to talk to him," Pete commented finally after listening to Marty's reasoning along these lines, "but it would have to appear to be casual."

"Why don't you go down to watch him practice ball?"

"Tonight?"

"No, I don't suppose that he was planning to take that blonde bomb to ball practice, but you could go tomorrow night. He lives and breathes basketball all winter."

"If it works out, I might do that."

The conversation drifted away to lighter subjects again and, as their path brought them near the house once more, Marty began to hopefully maneuver for a possible good-night kiss. Her plans were crushed instantly as Pete broke into a light run, pulling her along behind him, and chiding her:

"Come on, slowpoke, or we'll miss the annual TV version of Dickens' *Christmas Carol.*"

Marty laughed and admitted inside that she was satisfied with the day's progress without anything more.

* * *

Santa Alberta maintained within its city limits two versions of Hoover High School. When construction on the new school had been completed two years earlier, the older campus had been converted into offices for the board of education and district library. The old gym had been turned over for city-league play, and teams such as Bud Bailey's Blue Raiders called it their home court. League games had been suspended for the week between Christmas and New Year's, so on the night of December 26th only the most faithful "gym rats" showed up to work out. Al Stoddard emerged from the dressing room and was disappointed to discover that most of the regulars had found more interesting ways to pass the evening. He sat down on the bottom plank of the bleachers to relace his shoes. The gym was stuffy tonight, and the dimming lights that should have been replaced weeks ago made the atmosphere all the more depressing.

"Is this a closed session or can just anybody work out?"

Al looked up, startled by the newcomer who had just entered by the side door. "No, it's OK. We need everybody we can get tonight. There are dressing rooms at the other end if you want to change."

"I didn't bring anything along but shoes. Your sister-in-law told me that I might get a chance to play a little down here."

"Marty?" Al asked with surprise.

Pete nodded.

"Oh, you're the guy that's down here from her school."

"Pete Bradley's the name," he said, offering his hand.

"Yeah, glad to meet you. I'm Al Stoddard, but I guess you already knew that."

"It's written on the back of your sweat shirt."

"Forgot about that," said Al with a foolish grin. "Say, you and Marty been going together very long?"

"We're not really going together. I was stuck with a job up at school over the holidays, and she just felt sorry for anybody spending Christmas alone, so I got an invitation out of it."

"Yeah, maybe," said Al, looking wise, "but you'd better watch it with Marty. She knows how to play it around guys, and then just usually leaves them hanging."

"I can believe it," said Pete with a smile.

"Put your shoes on and come on out," Al directed, getting up off the bleachers. "We'll probably just play half court—three-on-three it looks like." He trotted out to the free-throw line to pick up a loose ball which he fired up against the backboard. Pete quickly laced on his tennis shoes, stripped off his outside shirt and joined the others in warming up.

"Hey, you've played before!" shouted Al after Pete had sunk two twenty-foot jumpers in a row.

"A few years ago—in high school."

"Don't they have a team at that school you go to?"

"They have one, but it would cut into my working hours too much if I went out."

"That's still a pretty shot," commented Al with admiration. "How 'bout you and me and Frank over there standing Wilson and his buddies?"

"Fine," Pete agreed.

With the sides determined and a game "to thirty" agreed upon, the action began. The six young men, playing at one end of the deserted gymnasium, their shouts and the occasional slamming of the backboard punctuating the methodical slap-slap of the ball on the court, provided the gloomy scene with warmth. Pete found himself able to hit with surprising accuracy from outside, and he and Al combined to swamp the other team in the first two games. The arrival of three other fellows forced them to switch to playing full court, but the results were unchanged.

"Pot another one—don't pass off when you're clear!" Al yelled at one point, and Pete obliged by missing the backboard entirely.

"Luck's finally run out!" he shouted back.

"Keep putting them up there. What you don't hit, I can tip in."

Two sweat-soaked hours later they quit, and Pete took advantage of a shower in spite of his lack of a fresh change of clothes. Feeling refreshed, he picked up his shoes and dirty T-shirt and headed toward the exit and the parking lot. He was relieved when Al caught up with him.

"Wish you'd be available to play when we start back on the regular schedule," Al said as they pushed open the heavy door and stepped into the night air.

"I might not be so lucky another time."

"Yeah, well I'd still like to have a soft touch outside the key like you've got."

Pete laughed as they crossed the parking lot. "I spent a lot of time on that shot, but it isn't doing me much good now." He opened the back door of his car and tossed in his bundle of T-shirt and shoes.

"Say, Pete, I've been wanting to ask you something all evening, though maybe you don't know anything about it."

"Go ahead."

"Well, did you happen to notice whether Joyce was upset after I was over at her folks' place yesterday?"

"You mean because you had that girl out in the car?" said Pete, getting right to the point. "Yes, I'd say she was upset."

"It was a pretty crummy thing to do, wasn't it?"

"You know it was without me saying so, Al. And you know you're not doing right by Joyce and Danny either."

"Right? Who knows what's right anyhow?" Al asked, kicking at the dirt. "This setup doesn't look 'right' to you, but the way we were living wasn't right to me either. It all just depends on how we look at it; nobody can say what's right or wrong."

"The Bible does."

Disgust began to breed in Al's expression. "A preacher," he sneered. "I should have known, but you seemed like a pretty good guy out there playing ball tonight."

"You're frosted off just because I said that the Bible teaches the difference between right and wrong?"

"The Bible and whatever's in it have nothing to do with my life. If Joyce hadn't gotten on that religion kick we might still be together."

"Then the Bible and what's in it do have something to do with your life, don't they?"

"Listen, Pete, save all the cute explanations for your professors. I'm just not the type for churchgoing."

"I never mentioned churchgoing, did I?"

"No," Al admitted.

"All I really want to say is that no matter what kind of mess you're in, Jesus Christ is the answer. Most of our difficulties stem from the fact that we're far away from God, and Jesus Christ is the only way back."

"Yeah—sure, sure," Al said, dismissing the subject. "Sorry, buddy, but religion just doesn't interest me at all."

"I'm talking about Christ—not religion."

"It's all the same to me."

Pete reached into his shirt pocket for a tract. "At least read this sometime for me, will you?"

"I don't read much."

"That won't be any big strain."

"OK," Al agreed in order to be done with the conversation. "If you ever come back to Santa Alberta, come on down to the gym again. I enjoy whipping Wilson and his friends."

"Sounds like a winner," grinned Pete, crawling in behind the wheel. "Good night, Al."

"Yeah, see you sometime," Al replied with a wave and sauntered over to his own vehicle.

Pete drove through the silent streets thinking about what had transpired during the evening. He was grateful for the opportunity that had opened up, and he thanked the Lord for it right then, and it was good that Al had taken the tract. Patience, perseverance and prayer—that was what was needed now. Al had not seemed to be the monster he had been led to expect. *Been listening to too many women,* Pete thought as he neared the Miller residence. *They never see anything straight.* With this as his concluding statement in the crosstown soliloquy, he parked the car behind Mrs. Miller's Chevy and, after locking the doors, went inside. Marty was waiting on the couch, eager and expectant.

"Well?" she said hopefully.

"Had a real nice time," he answered, sitting down next to her.

"You were able to lead him to the Lord?"

"Marty!" he said, astonished at her presumption. "You sure were expecting a lot for one evening."

"Well, I've been praying about it ever since you left."

"Marty, Marty," he said, putting his arm around her shoulder and forgetting his tirade against women. "It doesn't come that easy very often. But I think your prayer had results. I was able to talk to Al about the Lord for a while and I left a good tract with him."

Disappointment was written on her face. "But he's been talked to before. I hoped you could really nail him down and apply some pressure."

"That kind of pressure has to come from the Spirit working in his heart, and it takes time."

"And what's Joyce supposed to be doing in the meantime?"

"Wait it out, I guess. We just can't set up a timetable for God and expect Him to follow our orders."

"I suppose you're right," said Marty more sweetly. "I'm just disappointed that it couldn't have all been settled tonight." She leaned her head against his shoulder and sighed. "Thanks for trying anyway."

He smiled, amused by her innocence and touched by her sincerity. "Psalm 27:14 says: 'Wait on the LORD: be of good courage, and he shall strengthen thine heart: wait, I say, on the LORD.'" And without waiting any longer, he kissed her firmly.

5

Pete

MARTY TURNED OVER and tried to bury her head deeper in the pillow. For two hours she had been more or less successfully ignoring the hunt-and-peck symphony Jeanne had been playing on the typewriter. But, with the afternoon almost gone and her planned nap only a crushed hope, irritation was beginning to triumph.

"For heaven's sake, Jeanne, what are you doing anyway?" The words lashed out with more force than she had really intended.

Jeanne looked up placidly from her project, failing even to notice Marty's first display of temper in almost a month. "Oh, it's nothing, really," she said lightly.

"Then why did you have to pick Sunday afternoon to do it?"

"Have I been bothering you?" she asked innocently. "You should have said something earlier. I could have gone down to the lounge."

"Skip it," replied Marty with resignation. "I just can't figure why now that semester tests are all over, you suddenly get a bug to work. You should have been this industrious last week."

"Oh, this has nothing to do with school, or at least nothing to do with my grades. Mr. Lawrence asked me to take the transcript from the tape of his lectures on Eliot and do whatever editing and rewriting was necessary to put them in readable form."

"What's he paying you?"

"Nothing."

"Nothing!" Marty echoed. "You're doing all that work for nothing? Why?"

"I like it," she replied quietly, "and then I was very flattered that Mr. Lawrence thought I was capable of handling it. He could have gotten some senior English major if he had wanted to."

"What's Lawrence going to do with these polished gems of yours?"

"He's going to try to get them published."

"Will you get any credit?"

"Oh, I don't expect anything like that."

"Maybe it's smart not to expect things," said Marty moodily. "Then at least you can't be disappointed."

Jeanne turned away from the desk, taking in Marty's dismayed expression, but reluctant to ask about the problem. Trying to avoid the issue directly, she queried, "Are you taking the bus to church tonight?"

"Looks like it, doesn't it?" was the sullen reply.

"Pete didn't call?"

"Nope, Pete didn't call." Marty rolled out of bed and wearily walked to the closet. "For all I know he's through calling."

"Oh, Marty, I'm so sorry you two are fighting."

"Fighting?" sniffed Marty. "That's a laugh! He's not interested enough in me to even bother fighting. For the last two weeks he's acted like I didn't even exist. You know what he said at dinner this noon? 'See you tonight probably.' That's really something to build dreams on, huh!"

"But everything seemed so great for you right after Christmas vacation."

"Yeah, that's what I thought too." Marty laughed cynically. "Jeanne, if I just knew what I'd done or said to make him change this way. But I don't—I can't think of a thing! He's so cold and distant now—" She took her gray suit off the hanger and surveyed the press critically.

"The Lord knows all about it," Jeanne reminded her.

A lot of good that does me, Marty thought, and then was instantly ashamed. She made a silent petition for forgiveness and then smiled at her roommate. "That's an overworked cliché, but you're right, and thanks for saying it. I'm going down the hall to press my suit; can I do something for you at the same time?"

"Well, my green skirt is a little wrinkled," she began.

"OK."

"Have you eaten your sack lunch yet?"

"Didn't get one. I've had all the 'cheese and pimento on wheat' I can take."

Jeanne's mouth dropped. "You're not going to eat anything?"

"Not unless Bobby Jordan invites me out for a steak dinner after church." Marty grinned.

"Do you think he might?"

"No, silly. Get back to your project for Mr. Lawrence while I hunt down the iron. I feel reckless enough to treat you at the Dairy Freeze if the bus stops there afterward."

"Oh, it always does," responded Jeanne a little too eagerly. She watched Marty vanish out into the hall and tried to understand her friend's current wound.

* * *

Coastal Bible College offered bus service into Harwood on Sundays for those needing transportation. It was inevitable that the bus would be known as the "Old Maids' Wagon," and equally inevitable that some girls would feel they had been issued lifetime passes. The regular riders were able to board and depart without particular show of concern or embarrassment; only the newcomer or the occasional refugee gave indication of the loss of pride involved. Marty had not given the matter much thought before, but this was the first time in over two months that Pete had left her to her own devices for getting to church.

So she was very conscious of the surprised glances when she alighted in front of Harwood's Community Bible Church. Mechanically she checked the parking lot for the familiar white Falcon. It was there in the usual spot. Everything was really quite normal, she admitted to herself, suddenly realizing that Jeanne was waiting by the entrance.

They went inside and took seats near the back of the sanctuary. Pete's blond head was visible in a row of fellows toward the front. Marty had expected him at least to look around when the influx of bus riders arrived. He did not. Rather, he continued to exchange remarks with his roommate Jerry Amos who was sitting on the aisle. Jeanne tried to draw Marty's attention away by pointing out that Miss Hawley was sitting next to a thin little man with glasses.

"That's her brother from Arkansas!" prompted Kathy Mc-Masters who had just squeezed in at the end of the pew. She noticed Marty with surprise. "Hey, what are you doing—"

Jeanne shook her head as a warning for silence, but they both observed that Marty had not been paying attention.

"I'll tell you later," Jeanne whispered, and Kathy nodded with understanding.

The choir filed into the loft, followed by Reverend Carding. A dynamic man, equipped with a resonant voice and seemingly unlimited vocabulary, the pastor of the Community Church also doubled as a Bible instructor at the college. Jeanne found him impressive and often quoted maxims from his lectures; but he did not rank as one of Marty's favorites, either in the classroom or in the pulpit. Tonight she found it difficult to concentrate as he unwound a detailed outline of Ephesians 2. Her thoughts had jumped ahead of the clock, and she too was outlining, in this case her postbenediction strategy. She studied Pete carefully, hoping to note some sign that he also was bothered and unable to follow attentively. Distressed, she realized that he was not only listening but even making notes. *Two can play that game,* she determined inwardly, wondering how to make a game out of something that he didn't even regard as intentional.

The evening service seemed to drag on longer than usual. Marty knew that the Lord could not be very pleased with her inattention, but the guilt was somewhat rationalized when Reverend Carding, though apologizing in the process, ran ten minutes beyond the eight o'clock hour. Almost before the final amen had echoed back to their seats, Marty was on her feet and hurrying her complacent roommate out into the aisle. Kathy drew back to avoid being trampled and shook her head sympathetically. Marty's interesting behavior was attracting notice from all corners, but she succeeded in escaping through a side exit and reaching the shelter of the bus before most of the congregation had even replaced their songbooks in the racks.

"Marty," Jeanne said breathlessly as she dropped into the seat, "how is Pete supposed to be friendly when you don't even give him a chance to say hello?"

"I don't want to give him a chance to walk by the whole bunch of us and just wave and say, 'Hi girls,' either." The words tumbling out revealed that Marty lacked her normal preciseness and penchant for logic. The hurt was showing, and it was impossible to keep Jeanne unaware, though Marty would have preferred to have done her suffering alone and without consolation. *That's the trouble with ever caring too much about anyone or anything,* she thought. *It leaves you wide open.*

Slowly the bus refilled, certain girls lingering to the last minute in hope of receiving a more interesting offer. "Give it up, Corrine," called Sally Hoving over her shoulder as she mounted the steps. Corrine, who up to that time had been stationed on the sidewalk leading to the parking area, feet planted wide apart as if she were almost defying her prey the opportunity of passing her by, turned and glared viciously at the busload of girls watching her. With a determined toss of her head, she walked directly over to Pete's car and got in.

"I don't believe it!" said Sally to no one in particular.

"He couldn't have!" added Jeanne.

"Maybe Jerry asked her," prompted someone in the rear.

"I can't believe it even of Jerry!"

The lumbering yellow vehicle, with "Coastal Bible College" proudly emblazoned on both sides, pulled away from the curb and began its prescribed route home. Some of the girls applauded happily when it made the likewise prescribed detour to the Dairy Freeze. Marty was reminded of the kiddie pony rides at the zoo back home. The youngsters were thrilled with the thought of guiding a horse around the track but, in truth, the animals would have moved in the same direction and at the same pace regardless of the rider. She was depressed beyond what she knew to be right and found solace only in leaning her face against the chilled windowpane and allowing the familiar scenery to drift past her misty vision.

Jeanne watched for a while, wishing to comfort but feeling it ridiculous to say that she understood. She didn't, of course, understand what it was like to have a promising romance disintegrate at its seams; none of her "romances" had ever reached a point where it was possible to say that it had fallen apart. The feeling of rejection, however, was not unfamiliar and, even coming from such an enviable source, Jeanne knew the sickness that was a part of it and recognized the symptoms on Marty's face.

"Since this is your treat I'd better take advantage and try a double chocolate shake," she said finally as they pulled in behind the Dairy Freeze.

"Whatever you want," Marty replied halfheartedly.

"Well, come on. Let's go before too many get in line ahead of us."

Marty's dark eyes darted over the assemblage of parked cars; she decided it was safe. The two girls walked over to the line which had formed in front of the window and waited their turn. Jeanne sensed Marty's concern and, without saying anything, assumed her share of scanning the parking-lot entrances for the white Falcon. It appeared just as they placed their order; Pete and Corrine were alone in the front seat.

"She must have paid him," Jeanne whispered, and Marty reluctantly smiled.

Enjoying her moment of glory, Corrine was talking with animation as they joined the rest of the after-church crowd. Pete looked around uncomfortably, at the same time continuing to nod whenever she paused for an affirmation. Jeanne watched and reported the play-by-play account to Marty who was concentrating on the minute details of how their order was being filled.

"He's coming up here," she suddenly announced in an excited whisper, as Pete excused himself from the loquacious Corrine. Marty had handed the attendant the right change and had started to pick up the two shakes when she felt a hand on her shoulder.

"Is there any chance that I could take you home?" he asked quietly.

She turned and stared at him without comprehending. Finally finding her tongue, she said evenly, "It looked like you already had a full car."

Pete grimaced. "She was waiting in the car. What was I supposed to do? Anyhow, she just asked if I'd give her a ride over here, and I've fulfilled my part of the agreement now. She can take the bus the rest of the way."

"I thought maybe you were getting some spiritual counsel."

"Don't be sarcastic, Marty," he cautioned. "It doesn't look good on you."

"And don't you start lecturing me," she replied angrily, stepping aside to allow the waiting line to move up. Jeanne followed, listening and not knowing whether to collect her chocolate shake and tactfully disappear or not.

"Would you ride home with me so we can talk?" Pete asked.

Marty hesitated and looked around at her roommate as though seeking advice.

"Wait in the car," he directed. "I'll buy Corrine a sundae and tell her she has to find another way back, OK?"

Marty walked away without replying. "God's gift to women," she muttered.

"You've got to go with him," prompted Jeanne who was just a step behind.

"I don't have to do anything."

"At least give him a chance to explain."

"What difference does it make to you?" Marty snapped. "If he's through with me, maybe he'll take you out." Jeanne's round face dropped, and Marty hated herself. "I'm sorry, I didn't mean that," she added quickly, knowing that the damage had already been done.

"Well, now that's an idea," Jeanne said gaily, trying to carry it off, "but you go find out if it's really all over first, huh?" She took one container from Marty's hand and walked toward the bus.

"Thanks, roomie," Marty called, hoping that Jeanne would understand how very much she meant it.

It took Pete another ten minutes to get his order and an additional five to dispose of Corrine. Marty was sitting with a half-finished shake on her lap when he approached the car.

"You through?"

She nodded and watched him dump the remainder in the trash receptacle. He fished in his pocket for the keys, crawled in beside her, and started the car. They pulled out into the traffic, leaving several of their fellow students smiling at the evening's drama. Pete made a sharp right and headed onto the back road from Harwood to the campus. He made no effort at conversation but pushed the speedometer up to sixty, which for his car was nearly capacity. Marty sat and waited.

The road was almost deserted, and the little farmhouses along the side were already darkened in recognition that dawn was not too many hours away. Approaching the fork, Pete slowed down and then pulled off on a cow path to the left.

"Where are we going?" she asked, surprised.

"To an old haunt of mine." He guided the car around several bends and through a small gateway.

"It's a cemetery," she said in astonishment.

"Uh-huh," he replied, shutting off the ignition.

"Is this where you always take your dates?"

"Only when I want to talk to them." He leaned back against the door and faced her. "I guess you're wondering what's been the matter with me lately."

Marty was taken back by this direct statement and could only respond with a weak, "Yes."

"I got a letter from my folks last week. Dad's in the hospital again, and I've been trying to decide whether I ought to quit school and go home or not."

"Quit? When you're only one semester away from graduating?"

"That's what I thought too, but maybe it's what the Lord is asking of me. I really don't know at this point."

"But what about your brother who's in high school. Can't he help out until your dad's back on his feet?"

"Craig? Yeah, sure he could help out, but I told you he's been pretty sour on things for a couple of years. I don't know whether anybody can count on him."

"But surely under the circumstances—"

"Well, I hope so. Anyway, I told Mom I'd call tomorrow night. By that time the doctors are supposed to know a little more."

"What's the matter with your dad?"

"Kidney infection. He's had it before, but I guess there's some question of removing a kidney this time."

"That's too bad," was all Marty could say dully.

"So I've been kind of busy trying to get in a few extra hours of work, and I've had a lot on my mind. I didn't really ignore you on purpose."

"You make me look like a heel for getting my feelings hurt. Why didn't you tell me what was going on?"

"Didn't want to bother you with my problems."

"Well, I've sure bothered you with enough of mine over the last few months. Didn't you think it could work two ways?"

Pete smiled and drew her over to him. "Maybe I'm better at offering help than at asking for it."

"Please don't shut me out again," she murmured, her head resting against his chest to hide the tears.

He held her tightly for a moment. "I won't," he said quietly. "I can't."

*   *   *

Harrison Hall, according to the original building plans, had never been designed to have a chapel. The only room of any size was the cafeteria-dining area, which made it necessary to stack tables and set up folding chairs after each meal in order to convert the space into a lecture hall-chapel combination. Behind the lectern at the far end of the room a stained-glass window in the shape of a cross had been installed, and this served to remind the students that their purpose was a serious one even if the external surroundings were not always appropriate to conventional ideas of "religious" training. The ten o'clock hour was set aside for chapel, and as Marty rounded the corner coming from the library on that Monday morning she glanced up at the bulletin board to see what was scheduled for the week. It was with a decidedly different attitude than she had borne during the first few months of school that she took her assigned seat near the center of the hall. She eagerly anticipated the new semester, and the forty-five-minute worship services each mid-morning would be a refreshing break in the class schedule rather than the drudgery of before. Annette Perkins was playing an organ prelude while the student body settled down, and Marty searched the faculty and guest section in the front to try to pick out the day's speaker. The bulletin board had listed a foreign secretary from some mission agency. Though missionaries were not Marty's number-one choice as chapel speakers, at least this would be a welcome change from the over-supply

of Philippine Island appointees and those on furlough who had
spoken during the first semester.

The song leader stepped into position, and the service began:
three verses of a hymn, followed by prayer, and Dr. Todd's introduction of the speaker as an old friend from his seminary
days. Marty listened with casual interest as the short man with
a long-since receded hairline announced his topic as "Why Missions?" He had three clear points, and the curly haired fellow
sitting next to her was noting them in the flyleaf of his Bible:
"Because we love our fellowman; because the Word of God
commands it; because it provides an opportunity for us to glorify
God." Marty of course concurred with everything that was said.
Admittedly her interest in the subject of missions had grown
since she had learned of Pete's intention, but she still found the
idea remote and unrelated to her own life. The clock moved
slowly toward the 10:40 closing point.

"You who are sitting back in your chapel seats this morning
—waiting, perhaps even with apprehension, for a 'missionary
call' are to be disappointed if you limit God to visions or spec-
tacular illuminations. A young man who was later to lay down
his life for his God in a foreign country once said, 'A missionary
call is nothing more or less than obedience to the will of God,
as God presses it home to the soul by whatever means He
chooses.' The real question this morning is not *whether* God is
going to call some of you to foreign missionary service, but
what will be your response. In your hearts, are you asking your-
selves: Is there any reason why I should be a missionary? or Is
there any reason why I should *not* be a missionary?"

Marty sat forward in her chair, suddenly caught up in this
new line of reasoning.

"The second question," the speaker continued, "is more in
line with the clear teaching of God's Word. Now before you
walk out of this chapel saying, There's another guy telling us
we all have to go to the foreign field, I want to assure you I
have said nothing of the sort. But surely you cannot believe

God has called only those who have gone? Statistics reveal that 91 percent of Christian workers are serving in the 9 percent of the world that is English-speaking; and 9 percent of the workers are in the 91 percent of the world that is non-English-speaking. Ninety-six percent of every dollar given for the Lord's work goes to the efforts among English-speaking people. I say this not to minimize the need here in our own country, but to share with you this thought: Is our God so inefficient that this is His apportionment of workers and funds? Will you who have your entire lives ahead of you consider this? And will you allow God complete freedom to speak to your hearts? Shall we close in prayer."

Marty never heard any of the prayer. Her heart was beating faster than usual, and her brow was furrowed. Someplace down inside she was afraid he had been talking to her.

* * *

Headed for his one o'clock class, Pete waved at Dr. Herbert who was coming down the main hall. "How's Mrs. Herbert getting along these days?" he asked as they drew closer.

"Oh, better—a bit better," the old man replied absently.

"And you?"

"Oh, fine, just fine." With some effort Dr. Herbert managed to extract himself from his thoughts, and he faced Pete with an impish grin. "I'm on my way to a private conference with Dr. Todd. Maybe you ought to ask me that after I come out."

Pete smiled and patted the professor's arm. "I think you can take care of yourself in the lion's den." He said this with a confidence which he did not feel. There had been rumors going around since before Christmas that students had complained directly to the president about Doc's classes. Pete had heard Bobby Jordan spouting off in the dorm after dropping German I in order to maintain his eligibility, but no one took Jordan's gripes too seriously. Last week, however, when stories had crept out about an ill-prepared final exam and some unaccountable discrepancies in the grading of it, Pete had been concerned. He had intended to check in on Doc, but had become too entangled in his own difficulties to find the time.

"Come by and see us sometime, Pete," the professor said kindly, as if he had read the student's mind. "You'll have to excuse me now, or I'll be late for my appointment."

Dr. Herbert moved slowly down the corridor until he stood in front of the large door with the inscription "Office of the President." He was tired this afternoon and anxious to be done with the meeting. It was unusual that Ronald Todd had requested his presence at all. In recent years Dr. Herbert had relinquished his unofficial role as presidential adviser to some of the younger men and had come to look upon his full-time teaching load as quite sufficient responsibility. He rapped loudly on the door and entered.

"Paul, it's good to see you," greeted Dr. Todd heartily.

"Thank you for inviting me, Ronald."

Dr. Todd cleared his throat and looked uncomfortable. "Would you like a cup of coffee or something?"

"No, thank you."

"Paul, I know you're busy so I'll come right to the point. I find it rather difficult to begin in view of our long and pleasant personal relationship and your many years of service to the college. But there have been complaints brought to my attention recently regarding certain areas of your classroom procedure, and naturally we wish to investigate all sides of such allegations thoroughly and proceed. . . ."

Dr. Herbert had half suspected that this would be the basis for his summons, and it amused him to observe Todd caught up in his own eloquence, trying to ask a simple question. He was still the same little Ronnie Todd that Paul had known in the years that Dr. Todd, Sr., had pastored the Lakeside Avenue Church in Los Angeles. Little Ronnie had solemnly dogged his father's footsteps on all occasions, and he was still trying to fill shoes that stubbornly remained a size or so too large. Paul smiled at the remembrance of a reception for the Todds when—

Dr. Todd, now grayed and distinguished by several academic degrees, sat on the other side of the desk apparently waiting for a reply.

"I'm sorry, Ronnie, would you mind repeating that?"

The president looked on his colleague with astonishment, possibly because no one had called him "Ronnie" in thirty years, but also that the older man had neither heard nor understood the charges that had been made. "I said," he repeated with a strain of impatience, "among other things, that I have on my desk a petition signed by eleven members of your German I class complaining that material on the first semester's final had not been previously covered in class, although they concede that it was included on the original outline for the course. They state further that you are three weeks behind the outlined schedule, and I have also a folder of graded tests showing a lack of a consistent standard for marking errors."

"That class has been unhappy ever since they enrolled," said Dr. Herbert, trying to laugh. "I wouldn't worry too much about their complaints."

"Paul, I'm sorry, but I have similar petitions from French I and II and some isolated cases as well. Their charges seem to be well documented."

"Well, I suppose it's possible that I was a little careless. What with Frieda being under the weather and all, I just used a test from last year to save going out and having a new one mimeographed. Guess I did forget that this year's class hasn't been moving along as fast as I had intended."

"None of your classes has reached the halfway point in the courses, yet we're already into the second semester."

"Oh, Ronald, you know how it is with the kids these days. They are so busy doing things outside class that they just can't keep up. Why I can remember my last year at the university that we were required to—"

"Paul," Dr. Todd interrupted, "the students say that the

classes are behind because you repeat material in your lectures and get sidetracked with too many stories."

Dr. Herbert reddened and looked away. He didn't want any unpleasantness. "All right," he agreed finally. "I'll see that it's all business from now on, and I'll recheck the grading on those papers."

"We discussed this matter somewhat at our trustees' meeting last week," the president continued as though Dr. Herbert had said nothing in the interval. "And the general consensus was that, in view of your wife's health, perhaps we should consider granting you a leave of absence next year. That way you would be better able to care for her and possibly would have time to begin work on a book of your own or something. I personally feel that you could make a significant contribution in the area of the organization and administration of a Christian school. So if it meets with your approval we could put this suggestion in the form of a motion at the next meeting, and you could look forward to some well-earned vacation."

"Just like that," Paul Herbert said softly. "You'll probably even give me a testimonial dinner."

Dr. Todd sat dumbly, unsure whether he had succeeded in tactfully dropping the ax or not.

"I've always prayed that the Lord would grant me the grace to know when my usefulness in His work was over," the white-haired man continued with unwanted tears brimming in his clear gray eyes. "If that time has come, then I'll not oppose any action by the trustee board. Do you wish me to finish out this year?"

"We sincerely hope this will be possible. It will be extremely difficult to replace you at any time; practically speaking, it would be impossible at midterm." Dr. Todd watched the older man's face and ached inside for him. Authority seemed to bring more than a rightful share of distasteful tasks, and Ronald Todd also ached for himself as he pictured a similar scene in another twenty or twenty-five years. *I only hope I can do as well,* he thought.

"Was there anything else?"

"No, I don't think so. You do understand, don't you, Paul?"

"Yes, I understand." Dr. Herbert worked himself up to a standing position, shook hands cordially, and left the office. His step became a shuffle when he reached the hall, and he passed through the building without noticing any of the students lounging in the halls.

At least I won't have to tell Frieda—she'd never remember anyway, so there'd be no point. His mouth moved with these words, and for the moment he envied his wife's peaceful adjustment to a world of pain and hurt.

* * *

Though it had been on his mind all day, Pete delayed making his phone call until after 7:00 P.M. when the rates went down. With a pocket full of coins he approached the pay booth located in the corner of the Harrison lounge. It wasn't a particularly satisfactory arrangement for long-distance calls, and he hoped the connection on the other end would be good. He gave the operator the number, deposited enough change for three minutes conversation, and waited.

"Hello?" The voice on the line was thin and faint.

"Mom?"

"Yes? Oh, Pete! Oh, I'm so glad you called, son."

"What's the matter? Is Dad any worse?"

"No, no—he's really getting along better than we had hoped. The doctor said this morning that if he continues to improve he can come home Wednesday or Thursday."

"Hey, that's wonderful. Then everything's going along pretty well."

"Oh, we're a little messed up here around the place, but Craig's been a real help to me, and we ought to be able to manage until Dad's back on his feet."

"Well, praise the Lord," said Pete with relief.

"We're in His hands, and a few testings are no doubt for our own good. Anyway, you don't need to worry about coming home, son."

"Well, it'd be nice to see all of you, but I'd prefer to bring that diploma home with me."

"We can understand that. Uh, Pete—" She hesitated. "There is one thing that you need to know, and I don't know how much it will affect your plans. We had to pay the hospital bill with the money that was to have been for your tuition. I hope you've been able to put some aside from your work to make up for this. Maybe we can help out a little later on, though you probably shouldn't count too much on it."

Pete's heart sank. "Don't worry about it, Mom. I'll take care of things."

"You usually do, and we're very proud of you for it."

"Well, I don't want to run up too big a bill," he said briskly, "so tell Dad I'm praying and take care of yourself too."

"I will."

"Give my love to Craig, Ruthie and Sherry. Good-bye, Mom."

"Bye."

He replaced the receiver and sat stunned in the tiny enclosure. *I should have known they'd have to use that money. I should have known,* he thought dejectedly, the bill from the comptroller's office weighing heavily in his pocket.

* * *

Al had been perched atop the highest plank in the bleachers for a little over two hours watching the early qualifying rounds of the tournament. He had a thermos of coffee and some empty hamburger wrappers beside him, and at the moment he could even wish he was back eating Joyce's cooking again, as bad as it had usually been.

The team in the orange jerseys executed a perfect fast break, and Al made a note of it on the shot chart he had been keeping. Normally Bud ignored his collection of charts and plays, but possibly since this was tournament time and the results would determine whether the team would make the trip to Las Vegas, even Bud might be interested in having all the available information. The referee's whistle signaled the end of the third quarter, and Al looked around for the rest of his teammates. It was time for them to suit up, but only Harry Ranconi, another "outsider," had arrived at the gym. Arranging his charts on the clipboard and picking up his faded maroon field bag, the last remnant of his successes with the Santa Alberta Panthers, Al slid over to the edge of the bleachers and, using the guardrail, swung down to the floor. He pushed past the crowd of hangers-on that always gathered outside the locker rooms and went inside. The narrow dressing area was steamy and rancid-smelling in addition to being overcrowded. Al changed into his blue and gold suit as quickly as possible and was halfway through with the ankle-taping process when Bud and the rest of the fellows made their appearance.

"Make way for the soon-to-be-crowned city-league champs!" Bailey announced, and received the expected reaction of several well-aimed wet towels. "Hey, look at Al the early bird! Man, it must be great to grow up to be a professional gym rat!"

Al took the needling with apparent good humor, wishing at the same time that he had some kind of a comeback.

"This is the one we've been waiting for," said Bud, rubbing his hands while the fellows were dressing. Mentally he was checking the presence of each of his players. He stopped suddenly and whirled around. "Hey, where's Davis?"

The men looked at one another with puzzled expressions. "He said he'd be here in plenty of time," commented someone from the opposite corner.

"Plenty of time!" Bud exploded. "We're supposed to start warming up in a few minutes! How are we supposed to take First National without our big man—huh?? Any one of you blockheads got any bright ideas?"

The room was quiet. Even the players from the other teams joined in the embarrassing silence. Bud muttered several choice expletives and slammed his first into the side of a metal locker.

"Somebody's got to go look for him," he said through his tight lips while looking over the players grouped around him. "Al, put on your clothes and see if you can hunt him down."

"Wait a minute," Al protested, "I've been here since seven. Let somebody else do it."

"What do you think I'm doing—giving prizes to whoever sits around the gym the longest? Get going or you don't play to-night."

"No," Al retorted stubbornly.

Bud turned on him fiercely. "You must really think you're something—well, let me be the first to tell you, you're not! We need Davis all right, but we can get along without you any day. And if you don't do what I said and get started right now, you're through playing on any team I coach. Do you under-stand that, Stoddard?"

Al felt as though he were walking through a dream that per-sisted in turning out all wrong. He was uncertain of what to say next, but he wasn't going to take anymore of this off Bud. It wasn't worth it; even playing ball wasn't worth it.

"Are you going or not?" Bud shouted.

"No," Al answered quietly and began unlacing his shoes.

Bud spat on the floor at his feet and walked away. "Ranconi," he ordered, "go find Davis." Harry obediently reached for his clothes, and the rest of the team followed their coach out onto the floor.

"Don't let him get you down, buddy," commented a six-footer from the next cubicle. "Everybody in the league knows that Bailey plays favorites. You can probably hook on with some-body else next year."

"Yeah, sure," Al replied and concentrated on getting back into his street clothes. He gathered up his things as quickly as possible, stuffing them in the bag. The blue and gold jersey he left lying on the floor as a final gesture and, with head down, he trudged out through the swinging doors. None of his ex-teammates looked in his direction as he walked down the sideline toward the exit. It was not a very triumphant farewell.

The chilling February air greeted him outside, and it was a relief when the noises of the crowd died behind the heavy doors. The only others in the parking lot were people coming from night-school classes held in another building on the old high school campus. Al recognized a girl who had been a year or so ahead of him, and wondered vaguely what she was doing going to school again. "Maybe that's how I ought to be spending my evenings," he mumbled while standing in the dark beside his car. The idea struck him that it might be a way to show somebody something. He wasn't too sure who or what, but it was an idea.

*　*　*

Pete found that the baked eggs and burned toast offered for breakfast wouldn't go down. He returned his tray in its original condition and hurried out the side door. It was the wrong time of day and the wrong kind of weather for going up to the Lookout, but Pete felt he had to get away and spend some time alone with the Lord. Actually, he had spent most of the night alone with the Lord, but now it was morning and the answers were still not there. Walking along the lonely path, he was conscious only that the peace promised for all circumstances was not with him, and that he had to talk to someone in the business office before chapel at the latest. It seemed ironic in a way that the Lord could let him come this far, and then turn a deaf ear on his pleas for help. But that was how it looked on this winter morning. The school wanted to know where the money was for the new semester's bills, and he didn't even have enough to put gas in the car. He had read stories of God's miraculous provision under similar conditions, but there had been no mysterious letters in his mailbox this morning—he had checked first thing —and no one had pressed a check into his hand at breakfast. If God wasn't going to provide the sum, at least He might guide him in knowing what to say to the comptroller. Pete recognized that there was a strong trace of bitterness in his thoughts and, upon reaching the small summit, he flopped down on one of the log benches and buried his head in his hands. He prayed for nearly fifteen minutes without looking up. But when he did open his eyes, the world and his problems looked much the same. He contemplated sitting a while longer but decided that that would only be putting off the inevitable. Without further indecision he headed back to campus.

The door leading into the business office was ajar when Pete reached it. Mr. Farley, the comptroller, had arrived only a few minutes earlier and was sorting through items on his desk as Pete entered. He was an ordinary man, not the type generally cast as part of a college administration. The contact lenses which he wore were uncomfortable, and had it not been for his wife's urging he would have abandoned the attempt long ago. As it was he spent half of his waking hours squinting and the other half opening his eyes to their widest extremity. Jerry Amos had done a beautiful imitation of Mr. Farley at an impromptu talent show in the dorm last fall and, taking a seat in the business office that morning, Pete found it hard not to think of Jerry's performance.

"Bradley, Peter Morris, correct?" stated Mr. Farley, squinting.

"Yes, sir."

"You've come to make arrangements for paying your bill."

"I can't, sir," said Pete simply. "I don't have any money."

Mr. Farley's eyes opened wide. Pete hoped that it was from habit rather than particular horror at this last statement. "This is a serious matter, Peter."

"Yes, sir, I know it is."

"You can't even make one month's payment? We usually expect this as evidence of a student's serious intent."

"Mr. Farley, I have no money at all at this time. I'd been waiting to receive something from my folks, but this isn't going to be possible now."

"Well, it would be a shame for you to drop out in your last

semester. Isn't there some source from which you could borrow the money?"

"Not that I know of—unless there might be a school loan available," said Pete hopefully.

"I wish there were. What was left in the loan fund went to repair the gas lines in the kitchen. Coastal isn't what you might term 'well endowed.' "

Pete smiled. "Yes, sir, I understand."

The comptroller rested his chin in a cupped hand and frowned. A minute passed. "I'm not certain I have the authority to do this," he said kindly, "but let's give you another month to come up with something. Your record for payment in the past has been good, and I just can't see closing the door in your face when you're so close to graduation. Pray about it, work as much as you can, and then come see me around the middle of March."

"I appreciate your doing this, but frankly I can't see how I'll have the money next month either."

"There are a lot of things we can't see, Peter, and sometimes it's just as well. Fortunately God isn't limited by our vision."

"Thank you, sir," Pete answered, getting up from the chair and making his exit back into the hall. "It's in Your hands, Lord," he prayed briefly as he closed the door, but it was not easy to feel confident.

6

Dr. Herbert

THE REGULAR DRIVER of Coastal's station-wagon run into town had gone into service following the first semester, and Pete Bradley considered himself fortunate to have acquired the job. Aside from having to listen to the conversation of a carload of females, it was easy money and provided an hour's study time while the girls did their shopping. Today, however, he decided against studying and, leaving the wagon parked on the designated pickup corner, he walked two blocks toward the Herbert residence. Ambling along a side street, Pete tried to rationalize this visit as necessary; eventually he smiled at his own deception, knowing that he was counting on finding Marty there. He was almost certain that she stayed with Mrs. Herbert on Thursday afternoons.

The past week had been resplendent with unusually good prespring weather, and Pete and Marty had walked often in the fields and hillsides surrounding campus. Even now as he approached the house he knew that he shouldn't be wasting more time, and more importantly that he had no right to allow himself to be so interested in Marty—or any other girl for that matter, but it had never been a problem before. His life had enough complications at the moment without adding any of his own making, but nevertheless he was there and not about to turn around without a chance of talking to her. He walked up the front steps and rang the bell.

"Pete, my boy, come in!"

Pete was taken back at finding Dr. Herbert home, but recognizing the old man's genuine pleasure quickly covered his own disappointment. "I hoped I could borrow a couple of books," he stammered, coming inside.

"Certainly, but sit down. I was just getting ready to pour myself a cup of coffee. Will you join me?"

"Sounds good." Pete grinned. "Is your wife around?"

"Oh, she's out in the backyard inspecting the garden," the professor answered, returning from the kitchen with the coffee pot and two cups. His hands shook slightly as he filled the cups, but not more than usual.

"Yes, with this glorious weather we've been having Frieda's been so anxious to get outside. Of course it is a little early to do very much, but she enjoys it. And I don't think she's apt to get chilled this early in the afternoon, do you?"

"I wouldn't think so," Pete replied. "I was a little surprised to catch you home at this hour. Don't you usually have an afternoon class?"

"You mean you had expected to find Marty here?" Dr. Herbert asked with a twinkle.

Pete grinned and felt a bit foolish.

"No, I'm not teaching any classes in the afternoon this semester; in fact, the French II that normally met at this hour has been dropped from the curriculum until next fall."

"Why'd they do a thing like that?" asked Pete with exasperation.

"Mostly because none of last semester's students registered for the second half of the course."

Pete didn't know what to reply. He sat on the hard-backed chair and lamely looked around the room. Finally he met Dr. Herbert's eyes and observed in them the peace of understanding and acceptance. "I'm sorry about the problems you've been having," he said quietly, "and I want you to know that there are a lot of us who don't agree with what's been said or what's been done."

"Don't let it bother you, boy. We all have a few rough patches that show how much we're dependent upon the Lord, and how inadequate our own resources are. Am I right?"

"Yes, you are," Pete answered with his eyes lowered.

"I want to assure you, Pete, that I'm praying about your financial situation here at school. God has a purpose in all this, and I'm certain He has provision also."

"Thank you, Doc. I really appreciate it."

"I only wish I had the means to help you out, but don't give up hoping." Pete watched the older man's lined face as he spoke, and he hesitated before asking the question that had been on his mind the past several weeks. "But suppose God doesn't supply the money—suppose I can't pay the bill."

Studying the young man seated before him, Dr. Herbert wished there were the means of communicating years of experience to someone else. Words helped at times; occasionally counsel was accepted; but what was needed was the firsthand opportunity of seeing God work out His perfect plan apart from man's figuring and logic. And there was no way of acquiring this assuring knowledge except through experience in the Christian walk.

"Pete, you know that God expects faith on our part, but faith doesn't mean a blind trust that God will arrange everything to fit into our preconceived plans. He expects you to trust Him to work the situation out in such a way that it will bring the most possible glory to Himself, and I'm sure that's what you're really seeking."

"Yes," Pete admitted. "I ought to be looking at it from that view."

"I know it isn't easy, but keep in mind that God loves you. He isn't rejoicing in your bewilderment, only desiring to work out the attributes of Jesus Christ in your life. And sometimes the hard spots are the only means for bringing forth what God wishes to characterize your life."

It was quiet for several minutes as Pete allowed these words to sink in and soothe the resentment that had been building up inside. Finally he asked, "As long as we're on the subject of my life and its relationship to the Lord, Doc, what do you think I ought to do about Marty?"

"I didn't know that you considered Marty a problem," the professor laughed.

"I'm afraid I'm falling in love with her," Pete replied soberly.

"Well, Pete, you're what—twenty-one? Twenty-two years old? That's not such an unusual time for falling in love, and Marty is one of the most precious little Christians I've ever known. She's young in the Lord, but so deeply concerned about pleasing Him and knowing His Word. Why, I think 'falling in love' is a very good idea."

"But I can't even support myself—let alone two people. And I've got years of seminary ahead, and she's not through school either. And besides, I don't think she feels called to the mission field—at least not yet, and—" He paused in his intensity and realized that Dr. Herbert was smiling. For a moment it angered him, and then he too was amused by his own foolishness. "I know, I know," he said, "I'm trying to solve everything for the Lord and not allowing Him any space to work."

The old man nodded. "That doesn't mean that these aren't serious matters. They are—especially regarding your service for Him as a missionary if that is where He eventually places you. But one step at a time, OK?"

"OK," Pete agreed.

A door slammed in the kitchen, and Frieda peered hesitantly around the corner into the front room. Her face was flushed from the exertion, and Pete guessed that she was also quite tired.

"Hello, Mrs. Herbert," he said, rising.

She looked at him blankly.

"You remember Pete Bradley, don't you, Frieda?" Dr. Herbert interjected.

"Oh, yes, certainly," she said, beginning to smile in recognition. "You're Harold's friend from Chicago."

"He's a student here at the college, Frieda."

"It was nice having you with us," she went on. "Do come back again when you can stay longer." Taking Pete's arm, she escorted him to the front door. The professor gave him a helpless look and shook his head slightly.

"I have to get back to town before my station wagon passengers finish their shopping, Doc. Thanks for talking with me; I hope it did some good."

"Anytime, Pete. Anytime."

"Good-bye, Mrs. Herbert," he said as she urged him out the door. It closed swiftly behind him, and Pete carried his own problems with new humility the remainder of the day.

* * *

The women's dorm had been unusually active all afternoon. Since five o'clock the buzzer in the main hall had been signaling the arrival of the various floral deliveries, and excited squeals punctuated the air. Naturally not all of the girls were preparing to attend the homecoming banquet. Corrine Wright had borrowed a car and organized a bowling party for some of the "have-nots" of the dormitory. Across the hall from Corrine, Jeanne Robbins was squeezing into a pair of capri's with the help of Marty's critical surveillance.

"Do they look too tight?" she asked, having won the battle of the zipper.

"Try it with your blouse on the outside," Marty suggested. "Yes, that's a lot better."

"Do I really look OK?"

"Fine," Marty assured her, though mentally conceding that capri's did nothing flattering for Jeanne's roundness.

Jeanne looked at her watch, wound it, then began poking at her hair.

"Sit down," laughed Marty from her chair beside the desk. "You're going to be too worn out to last through the tennis game if you don't take it easy!"

Jeanne obediently sat down on the end of her bed, but still couldn't control the fidgeting. "I hope I don't play too badly," she said anxiously.

"Don't worry about it! It's not all that big a deal. Pete and Jerry are just going to take us to the Harwood courts for a couple of sets and then out for a coke or something. You'll do fine."

"But, Marty, do you realize this is my first date at Coastal? Even if Pete did arrange it, it's still pretty important to me."

"Good. I'm glad it is. But Jerry Amos isn't so special that you have to be scared spitless about spending an evening with him."

"I'm not scared," Jeanne defended herself. "Just a little nervous."

"Well, anyhow it's better than doing nothing on banquet night, and Pete's budget just wouldn't squeeze out the $8.50 for tickets. We'll probably have a bigger time anyway."

"Probably," said Jeanne, trying to sound confident.

The buzzer rang from downstairs, followed by a voice calling, "Marty Miller and Jeanne Robbins!"

"Come on," Marty directed her roommate who now seemed riveted to the bedpost. Jeanne stood up, took one last hopeful look in the mirror, and followed Marty out the door and downstairs. Pete and Jerry were waiting on the front porch.

"About time!" Pete teased. "Thought maybe you'd come up with a better offer for the evening."

"Well, we did have a couple," returned Marty, "but I was afraid a corsage might give me hay fever."

Jeanne and Jerry exchanged quiet "hi's," and the foursome got into Pete's car. From the front seat Marty glanced around to check on Jeanne's actions. Predictably, she was sitting as close to the window as possible. Equally predictably, Jerry was sitting stiffly in the opposite corner. *It may be a long evening,* thought Marty, and she wondered what sort of persuasion Pete had used to induce Jerry to come in the first place.

As Marty had feared, it did prove to be a long evening. Jerry and Jeanne did not make a successful doubles team, and after two lopsided sets they gave up and tried a small restaurant on the outskirts of Harwood. Jeanne, who had managed to forget some of her self-consciousness out on the courts, was suddenly overwhelmed by the obvious need for small talk. She seemed to finish each sentence behind the menu.

"What sounds good to you, Jeanne?" said Pete, trying to draw her back into the conversation.

"I—I haven't quite made up my mind," she replied quietly.

Jerry drummed his fingers on the table and looked around impatiently. He spotted two recent Coastal grads on the other side of the room and excused himself to talk with them for a few minutes. Jeanne watched his departure mournfully.

"What are you having?" she whispered to Marty.

"A cheeseburger probably. Just go ahead and order whatever you want, Jeanne."

"All right," she said and returned to a concentrated study of the menu. Pete and Marty exchanged glances, but neither knew how to control the situation.

Jerry returned at the same time the waitress arrived for their order. "Everybody got his mind made up?" he said, looking at Jeanne.

"I'll have a coke," she said, putting the menu down on the table.

"Is that all?"

"I'm not very hungry tonight."

Jerry shrugged his shoulders and turned back to the waitress. "Let me have a hamburger, fries, and a chocolate shake."

Pete ordered cheeseburgers and shakes for himself and Marty, and the three of them kept rapid-fire conversation going throughout the meal, while Jeanne carefully nursed her coke in order not to finish too quickly. Marty mentally wrote the whole project off as a lost cause and was actually relieved when they got back to campus and Jerry escorted Jeanne to the door. He said a brief good-night, waved at Pete and Marty, then cut across the grass toward the men's dorm.

Pete looked over at Marty and grinned, "No more playing cupid, OK?"

"They didn't exactly hit it off, did they?" she admitted.

"Well, we tried anyhow."

"Is that going to help Jeanne?"

"No, I suppose not," he replied, scooting the front seat back another notch and stretching his legs. "Man, I'm beat tonight." He yawned twice as evidence.

"Do you have to work all day tomorrow?"

"Yeah. But it's good—I need the hours."

Knowing his sensitivity, Marty hesitated to bring up the subject, but she finally asked, "Are you going to make the March 15th deadline?"

He didn't answer immediately. Concentrating his view on a crack in the ceiling of the car, he waited, almost as if hoping for some other answer. "Not without some kind of a miracle, I'm not," he said finally.

"I've been asking God for one."

Pete smiled. "I appreciate that, my little friend. Guess all we can do is wait and see."

"You're taking it all so calmly," Marty commented. "I'd be wild about this stage of things."

"I'm trying to put up a good front," he agreed and looked down at his watch. "Two minutes to go. Shall we pray about it all?"

To Corrine and her bowling partners who had just pulled into the parking spot behind them, the couple with bowed heads could easily have been sharing some sort of whispered secret. And when with wide eyes the girls took in the kiss that followed, it seemed certain.

"I'll bet they announce their engagement sometime this spring," Sally Hoving commented, getting out of the borrowed car.

"I think he'll see through her act before that," said Corrine loudly enough that Pete and Marty turned around at the interruption.

* * *

Marty didn't see Pete again until before supper the next evening. She had been waiting in the lounge, and immediately recognized from his expressoin that something new was troubling him. She held off asking until they were almost through with the meal, and the table they had chosen had been deserted by the other students.

"What's today's big problem?" she asked, pushing aside a dish of pudding.

"It shows that much, huh?"

"Well, it does to me, but then I watch you pretty closely."

"You'd better," he laughed. "I've really got the means to start impressing some other girl."

"You think I love you for your money?" she questioned. It was the first time she had ever used the word "love" even in kidding, and she watched him for some reaction. There was none. For all the progress that it seemed they were making, Pete was as carefully noncommittal as ever.

"I hope not! No, what came up today really isn't a problem —just a decision that has to be made."

"You don't have to tell me. It wasn't any of my business to ask."

"Oh, there's no secret about it. Dr. Todd asked me today if I'd be interested in taking over the leadership of a couple of boys' clubs in Harwood. They're run by a community social agency, and this is the first time the college has been given the opportunity of furnishing leaders."

"But you don't have time to do anything else!" she protested.

"No, I'd have to give up the gardening at the Grayson place

on Tuesday and Thursday afternoons. The boys' club work does pay a little, but not as much as working for the Grayson's."

"Then I don't see why it's such a hard decision."

"Well, Dr. Todd feels this could be a real opportunity for an outreach into the community, and he wants to have the right person in it to get things going."

"And I suppose you're the only fellow on the Coastal campus who's capable of doing the job correctly."

Pete smiled and even blushed a little. "That did sound pretty bad, didn't it?"

"Uh-huh."

"Oh, Marty," he said, scooting his chair back from the table, "I don't know. Maybe the Lord's testing me to see what really comes first in my life. Even with the Grayson job it looks impossible for me to come up with all the money I need—the room and board maybe, but not the tuition. Oh, Marty, sometimes I don't see why I don't just quit right now. It seems stupid to be knocking myself out for something that can't be done." His expression was hard. "If I wasn't trying to go to school I could manage a job and do the boys' work too."

"Could be," replied Marty with a deep sigh. "I wish I had the money to loan you."

"Then everybody would think I was after you because you're rich," he laughed. "I don't know. I have to give Dr. Todd an answer on Monday. Anyway, there are still a couple of weeks before I have to stand in Mr. Farley's office with empty pockets. I guess the Lord can provide if He chooses."

"Well, I hope He chooses."

"Come on," he said, standing up. "I'll walk you over to the dorm, then I've got to go prepare a Sunday school lesson for to-morrow. I've been promising the kids for two weeks that I'd have a chart of Paul's missionary journeys."

She picked up her purse and slipped her coat over her shoulders. "Couldn't you find a chart like that in the Christian Ed department?" She would have liked to have spent a couple of hours of this Saturday evening with him.

"I probably could have, but the room was all locked up when I got here tonight. Miss Griswold has the only key to the files anyway."

Marty conceded defeat, and they left Harrison and walked up the road to the dorm. At the door he squeezed her hand and said good-night. She went inside, disappointed but hardly in a position to complain.

"Hey, Marty!" Sharon Bates hailed her. "I was just going to look for you. You've got a long-distance call waiting!"

*   *   *

The small white room with its ordered arrangement of beds, nightstands and chairs had seemed large enough to Joyce on the preceding evening when she had finally been wheeled in and abandoned by the last of the nurses and aides. This morning, however, with the arrival of another girl, the walls appeared to have closed in. She rolled over with some effort and tried not to notice the young man who sat near his wife's bed, stroking her hand and smiling proudly. Their voices faded mercifully, and Joyce dozed until the nurse arrived to prepare all the new mothers for the ten o'clock feeding.

"Come now, Mrs. Stoddard, is it? You're going to have to wake up before that little lady of yours comes in." The white-uniformed girl filled a basin of water and laid it alongside the soap and washcloth on Joyce's table.

"They'll be bringing the babies in a few minutes." Turning to the occupant of the other bed, she commented briskly, "Mrs. Harris, we won't be bringing your little fellow in until the two o'clock feeding today."

Mrs. Harris, her thin blond hair disarranged over the pillow, nodded and then smiled weakly in Joyce's direction. "You have a girl, huh?"

"Yes."

"That's nice. Your first?"

"No, I have a little boy at home."

"Oh, that's good. I mean, men are usually so proud to have a son. My Jimmy is just so excited about Jimmy, Jr. Of course I'm sure your husband is thrilled to have a little girl now."

"Oh, yes," Joyce lied, wondering how much longer she could keep up the pretense. She was so tired of going through the motions for the benefit of all the onlookers, both the close observers and the casual ones like this Mrs. Harris. Her "brave Christian front" was developing some serious cracks in its foundation.

The nurse returned and deposited a pink-blanketed bundle in her arms. "Here's the formula. Now is everything all right?"

"Fine," Joyce replied without emotion.

The door closed and she was left with this red-faced infant at her side. The baby's eyes were dark, and her head was thatched with thick black hair. She was quiet although the little mouth was making sucking motions. Joyce really didn't feel like bothering, but mechanically and dutifully she forced the nipple into the small puckered opening. Seconds later her daughter responded by gasping and choking, and Joyce quickly replaced the bottle on the table and lifted the little bundle to her shoulder. The baby began to cry loudly.

"Having trouble over there?" asked Mrs. Harris.

Joyce ignored the question and tried again. The results were the same; and little Miss Stoddard balked on the third attempt also. Weary and upset, Joyce leaned back on the stack of pillows, allowing the crying baby to rest across her chest.

"You want me to ring for the nurse," the solicitous Mrs. Harris inquired.

"Yes," was the half-audible reply.

Minutes later the nurse popped back in the door. She surveyed the situation with evident disgust. "No luck? We'll have to try a little harder next time, won't we?"

We sure will, thought Joyce, and the successive thoughts drove her face into the pillow. *I hate her!* she sobbed. *I hate*

*everything she means in my life. O, God, it's too much. It's just
too much. I can't do it—I just can't do it!*

The remainder of the morning was a fog of answering questions, following instructions, and finally playing with a tray of
food. Then it began all over again with the doctor's visit, another feeding battle with the baby, and a rest period preceding
the official visiting hours. Joyce hoped that her mother would
wait until evening to come; she didn't feel like talking right
now. The arrival of Mrs. Harris' Jimmy, Sr., made the situation
all the more unbearable, and she again tried to shut out the
happy couple by turning her face to the wall and concentrating
on nothingness. So successfully had she mastered this trick, that
the deep voice nearby startled her.

"Joyce? Are you asleep?"

She turned over slowly, unbelieving. "Al! What are you
doing here?" she gasped.

"Reverend McCormick called me this morning and said that
the baby was here." He hesitated a little, "I—I thought I
should at least come down and take a look at her."

"You'll have to go down to the nursery to do that," Joyce
replied flatly.

"Yeah, I know. I'll go down in a few minutes. Uh—how are
you feeling?"

"OK."

"Not too rough this time?"

"No."

He stood at the bedside, looking down at her with discomfort.
Joyce wasn't sure whether she wanted to help him or not. Either
way, she didn't feel like making any more casual conversation.

"I—uh—brought you some flowers," he said, indicating the
waxed-paper-wrapped bouquet lying unnoticed on the dresser.

She raised herself up on one elbow and smiled for the first
time. He had even remembered her fondness for pink rosebuds,
and it was a pleasant sensation beyond words to be treated with

unexpected interest and tenderness. "I think there's a vase in the top drawer."

Al walked over to the dresser, found the vase, and filled it with water at the sink. "You want them over here or on your table?"

"Over there'll be fine."

Setting the vase down, unimaginatively to one side, ignoring the lace dresser scarf, he returned to the chair at the side of her bed. They looked at one another without speaking for some time. Surrendering to the pressure created by silence, Joyce assumed her customary role and asked politely, "How did your team come out in the tournament this year?"

"They won city, but got beat out in state," he answered without any particular show of enthusiasm. "I quit playing, you know."

She was surprised. "No, I didn't. Why?"

"Just got tired of it, I guess."

Joyce wanted to say something, to encourage him or whatever was needed, but her mind remained blank. She lay back on the pillows, uncertain whether "I'm sorry" was an appropriate comment or not.

"I've been taking some courses at night since I stopped playing," he continued.

Now her astonishment was beyond containing. "You have?" she said with a strong overtone of unbelief. "Are you going to try to get your diploma?"

"Ah, I don't know about that." He was embarrassed by the sudden attention. "I'm just taking typing and business math. Thought maybe I could qualify for something in the personnel department at Sealy's instead of having to work out on the floor."

"That's great, Al. I really think that's great!"

"Oh, it's nothing that much. I may flunk 'em anyhow."

"But at least you're trying."

"Yeah, Joyce. I'm trying," he said seriously. "That doesn't mean a whole lot—I mean, about us and all that. But I wanted to come here and see the baby, and I wanted you to know that—well, that I'm trying."

Joyce felt the muscles in her throat tighten. She reached over and took his massive hand in hers. "I'm glad you came," she whispered.

He shifted his position uncomfortably. "Guess I'd better get down the hall and see that little girl. What'd you name her?"

"Nothing yet."

"I saw a book in the drugstore the other day that had a whole bunch of baby names in it. Want me to get it for you?"

Joyce, aware that the library contained numerous such volumes, laughed and replied eagerly, "Maybe that would help."

"I'll try to get it this afternoon," he said, standing up. "Well, be seeing you, Joyce. Take care of yourself."

"OK." She smiled and watched him leave. The Harrises on the opposite side of the room displayed obvious curiosity, but Joyce was too contented to be bothered. *It didn't really mean anything,* she told her rapidly beating heart. *He just came by to see the baby, and he really didn't stay very long. And he's still Al—unpolished and ignorant in so many ways. But he's all I can hope for.* And for the moment she was satisfied to have at least an object of hope. It had been so dark for so long.

* * *

The delinquent cuckoo croaked seven times at ten minutes past the hour. Dr. Herbert reminded himself again that he really should get the clock into the repair shop. Carefully he made his way through the dimly lighted living room and cautiously opened the door into his wife's bedroom. She was asleep now, after having tossed restlessly most of the afternoon, but he was still concerned with the audible rattling in her chest. Listening to her breathe, he concluded that it was at least no worse than it had been earlier. *Probably just a touch of bronchitis,* he concluded, closing the door and returning to his easy chair. A Sunday evening at home was a rarity and, since it was excusable and justified tonight, the old man turned on the television and prepared to enjoy the lineup of Western programming. He lasted past the first two commercials before moving into a sound sleep.

*   *   *

On the following Wednesday Jeanne Robbins began the descent from her dream world of popularity and attention back to reality. Jerry hadn't called. In fact, she hadn't seen much of him since the preceding Friday night in spite of her well-planned efforts. She had allowed herself to hope that he might ask her to the men's open house that was scheduled for Saturday evening. Of all the events in the college year, this one held primary social importance, mainly because of the pressure placed on every one of the fellows to ask a girl. As a result about one hundred twenty-five Coastal girls had reason to celebrate, and about fifty others bore a heavier than usual stigma.

Jeanne paced around the strips of walking space in their room, waiting for Marty to get back from supper. If Jerry intended to ask her, he probably would have said something to Pete, and Pete probably would have said something to Marty, she reasoned. If he was going to ask someone else—well, then, she wasn't really any worse off than she had expected to be. This, however, was not much comfort. Jeanne sat down on the bed and tried to pray about it, knowing of course that she ought to leave the matter completely in the Lord's hands and forget it. But it really didn't seem like too much to ask—just one date for just one evening. She was figuring a way to word this request to God so that it wouldn't sound selfish, when her roommate breezed in.

"Ouf!" Marty exclaimed, dropping her books on the desk. "What a day! I just about missed the station wagon back from town at five o'clock, and I never did find the right card, but look what I got for my new niece." She dug out a sack from among the books and drew out a pair of blazing red tights with rows of white lace across the backside. "Think they'll fit?"

"They don't look big enough to fit anything human," said Jeanne, smiling.

"They're only a three months' size, but I wanted her to be able to wear them right away while it's still cold. Man, and it has turned cold again tonight!" Marty rubbed her hands vigorously. "I'd thought about going up to the library later, but think I'll stay home by the fire instead."

"You mean our popping and whistling radiator?"

"It's better than nothing. What have you been doing all day?"

"Not much," Jeanne answered honestly. "Where's Pete tonight?"

"He went down to the hospital again."

"Is Mrs. Herbert any better?"

"About the same, I guess. Pete says it's a shame that Doc didn't call a doctor before Sunday night. She was already pretty bad by the time they got her to the hospital."

"It's sort of hard to get old, I suppose."

"Uh-huh," Marty replied absently as she thumbed through her notebook . "Say, did Mr. Lawrence assign you guys a short story to write for some nutty contest? Mrs. Cunningham said we had to have something original and creative ready by Friday, and I can't find the notes on how long it was supposed to be."

"We wrote some stories for Lawrence a couple of weeks ago, and he said he was going to enter the best of those. I think they're supposed to be about fifteen hundred words long."

"Well, how long is that?"

"About five typewritten pages, double-spaced."

"Guk!" said Marty, collapsing into the chair. "I don't have five typewritten pages of originality and creativity in me! Come on, Jeanne, help me out. You're always reading some kind of story. Tell me something to write about."

"They say you're supposed to write about something you know."

"And when you don't know anything about anything?"

Jeanne laughed, "Sure, sure. That's why you make all A's!"

"That's different. I can learn what's in a book, but to just make something up out of nothing—"

"Write a love story," Jeanne ventured shyly. "Write a story about you and Pete."

"You're kidding! That would be impossible."

"Why?"

"Because I don't know how it's going to turn out."

"You're not supposed to be writing a full-length novel! Just take some little incident that makes a good story, and then change the names and the setting a bit."

Marty thoughtfully chewed on a ball-point pen. "You mean like: 'One night Horace and Henrietta went out on a date in New York. They went to a party at church, ate ice cream at the Freezy Dairy afterward, and came home. The end.' How was that?"

"You're not even being serious," said Jeanne, a little disgusted.

"But I really can't make up stories," Marty protested. "Tell me what you wrote about."

"Oh, I just used something that happened in high school."

"What?"

"I don't want to tell you all about it," Jeanne replied, backing off from the subject. "You can read it when Mr. Lawrence hands them back."

"That won't help me much tonight." She got up from the desk, kicked off her shoes and flopped on the bed. "I don't feel like writing anyway."

Jeanne hesitated to ask what was on her mind, but decided that knowing would be better than not knowing. "Did Pete happen to say whether Jerry has a date for men's open house yet?"

"You hadn't heard?" said Marty, sitting up again. "He asked Sharon Bates."

"I was just wondering," replied Jeanne as casually as she could.

Marty watched her with concern. "I'm sorry, Jeanne. It's only Wednesday, though. Maybe someone will still ask you."

The lines in Jeanne's usually soft and placid face hardened. "Do you really believe that, Marty?"

"Well, you never know." Marty was embarrassed to be put on the spot. "A lot of the guys will be asking someone."

"Why don't you just tell the truth for once, Marty, and stop saying what you think I want to hear!"

Completely taken back by this rare outburst, Marty sat by dumbly as Jeanne bounced angrily to her feet and stomped over to the window. Tears were silently rolling down her face.

"Do you want to talk about it, Jeanne?" Marty finally asked.

"It won't do any good," was the weary reply.

"It might." Marty waited, but Jeanne continued to stare fixedly out of the window into the early evening gloom. "If having a date really means this much to you, then maybe we ought to talk about it."

"It doesn't mean this much," the other girl denied. "At least it's not supposed to."

"Why not? Everyone else around the dorm worries about dates. Why shouldn't you?"

"Because I ought to be satisfied with what the Lord has given me."

"Well, maybe the Lord wants to give you something more."

"Then I ought to be satisfied to wait until He does," answered Jeanne, turning away from the window at last.

"Well, maybe He expects you to help Him out a bit."

Jeanne stared at her without comprehending.

"OK, OK. That's not the theology we learned in Bible doctrine class, but what I'm trying to say is that there's no need for you to make it so hard for the Lord to give you what you want."

"I don't want a date that badly."

"Now who's not being honest?" Marty interrupted. "Jeanne, if you'd trim off about twenty pounds, and start rolling your hair every night, and check the hem length on some of your dresses, there's no reason why you'd have to be sitting home on weekends."

"You'll guarantee I'd have dates?"

"No, of course not. But at least you'd know if you didn't it was because that was the way the Lord wanted it—not just because you were too sloppy and careless."

Jeanne pondered this suggestion, her feelings apparently uninjured by the frank appraisal. "It does sound reasonable," she admitted and headed out the door and down the hall to splash some cold water on her eyes.

* * *

The lights of the small café facing the main entrance of Drake Memorial Hospital in Harwood briefly reached out into the darkened street as the door opened and two figures left its premises. They crossed the street and stood momentarily in front of the fountain that dominated the hospital's front courtyard.

"You'd better get on back, Pete. I'm sure you have studies, and now that Elsa is here I should be able to get some rest."

Pete watched the white-haired man with sympathy. Dr. Herbert's face was gray and lined, and deep circles lodged darkly below his eyes. The arrival of Frieda's younger sister Elsa had indeed lightened the load somewhat, but not sufficiently to guarantee the rest that was needed. Pete was of course aware that his own presence was not of any great value, beyond that of assuring his older friend that someone shared the burden and concern, if only from a distant point of view.

Looking at his watch, he commented, "It's only nine. I can stay a while longer if you'd like to walk or just sit out here and talk for a bit."

The professor glanced anxiously up at the fourth floor. Most of the rooms were no longer lighted and, except for emergencies, the hospital had become quiet. "I should get back up there."

"Elsa's with her," Pete reminded him.

Dr. Herbert sat down on one of the stone benches placed on the perimeter of the fountain and thoughtfully studied the methodical rise and fall of the water into the lighted pool. "It can't be much longer, Pete."

Pete was surprised to hear this admission. For the past half hour as they had sat drinking coffee Dr. Herbert had talked of vacation plans for summer, even a trip back to the old country to visit some of the relatives Frieda had still living there. He had talked of plans for their garden and the hidden advantages retirement would bring. Now he was acknowledging that it had been only talk. What had been obvious to the doctors for the last two days was also obvious to the husband—time was running out. Pete had no idea what he ought to be saying as comfort or help. It seemed ridiculous for him to offer spiritual consolation to this one who throughout his four years of college had stood by and advised at every crisis. Feeling inadequate and disadvantaged by his twenty-two years, he sat down on the pool wall and stared down at the cement walkway.

"Don't feel so bad," said Dr. Herbert, noticing the boy's discomfort. "I'm afraid, but only for myself, not for her. You won't understand for many years, but the time will come when going home to be with our loving heavenly Father looks glorious indeed." The words were strong, but the human voice that carried them broke, and tears flowed gently from the old man's eyes. He made no effort to cover them, but smiled and said, "This is another benefit of growing older. You can cry without embarrassment, and everyone understands."

The minutes passed without further conversation. Pete felt as though he were being allowed to witness something that God intended to use for his own benefit, yet he was also conscious of being an intruder in one of the most difficult and heart-rending phases of another man's life. Dr. Herbert, however, was not thinking of what was presently transpiring. His mind had focused on a moment twenty years earlier when Frieda had remained at his side after the others had quietly departed from the little cemetery; together they had thanked God for the son He had given and then taken back so unexpectedly. This time he would stand alone.

"Please, Pete. Go on back to school. I'm going upstairs now."

Pete stood up, brushed his slacks, and said good-night. He walked quickly toward the parking lot, and Dr. Herbert made his way up the low steps and entered the building. A nurse on duty at the reception desk looked up and then turned back to her work. He crossed the lobby to a waiting elevator, pressed the button for the fourth floor, and for seconds felt shut away and protected in the small cubicle. Reaching the fourth level, the doors parted and, steadying himself somewhat, he stepped out into an almost deserted corridor. He walked with deliberation to the visitors' room. At the doorway he stopped. Elsa was seated on a hard, vinyl-covered sofa, her handkerchief to her eyes. The night nurse and Dr. Palmer talked quietly nearby. Paul Herbert braced himself and went inside.

* * *

Services for Frieda Herbert were held in the college chapel on a gray and drizzly day in early March. Two weeks later the weather was still damp and, as Pete returned to campus after a two-hour gardening session, he was fighting a natural depression. Hopes for extra hours of work had been spoiled by the persistent rain, and he was beginning to wonder whether he had been wrong in turning down the boys' club work. If the Lord had intended that decision as a test, then he had flunked flat. Pete banged his fist against the steering wheel. It was getting harder not to question the fairness of all this. Why did God make him sweat out every payment every year when a character like Bobby Jordan got a free ride with a basketball scholarship?

Pulling into the main gates of Coastal, he guided the car past the buildings and into the parking area. It was muddy as he stepped out; another of the school's projects when funds were available was the paving of the parking lot. Hurrying to avoid a complete soaking, Pete dashed up the hill and reached the protective arch of Harrison's,entrance. He scraped most of the mud off his shoes and went in. Marty was waiting by the bulletin board.

"Haven't you eaten yet?" he asked.

"Decided to wait for you. Had to read a couple chapters from books on the reserve shelf anyhow."

"Well, if you can stand waiting just a couple minutes more, I want to run upstairs and check the mail."

"At this hour? What are you expecting?"

"A notice from Mr. Farley."

"Oh," she replied sympathetically. "Well, I might as well go up with you."

They mounted the winding staircase to the second floor of classrooms. The far end of the hallway served as a post office, and as Pete approached the rows of gleaming metal boxes the gnawing in the pit of his stomach grew. A peek through the grillwork on his box revealed that there was something inside. He quickly dialed the combination, opened the box and withdrew a single envelope.

Marty's eyes phrased the unspoken question. He silently handed her the envelope. It was addressed simply to Peter Morris Bradley, with the upper corner identifying the sender as "Office of the Comptroller." She handed it back, and he held it up to the light.

"Surprise, surprise," he said bitterly and stuck the envelope into his shirt pocket.

"Aren't you going to open it?"

"It's just my bill," he said with a shrug.

"Well, if we walked all the way up here, the least you can do is look at it."

"Whatever you say," he replied in mock obedience and tore open the envelope. He took a quick glance at the billing sheet it contained, his eyes suddenly stopping at the bottom of the page. Pete stared with disbelief.

"Now what's wrong?"

Again he handed her the letter, this time pointing to the line in question. It was marked "Payments completed through April 1."

* * *

The mysterious answer to Pete Bradley's current financial need was shared with the entire student body during chapel the next morning. In the closely knit circle that enveloped the faculty, students and staff at Coastal it was reason for praise and rejoicing, although the human means which God had used in this answer to prayer remained a well-kept secret. Mr. Farley had originally intended to tell no one, in accord with the wishes of the donor. But following the chapel services he felt compelled to drop by Dr. Todd's office.

Ronald Todd was busy preparing an address he was scheduled to give that evening at a church banquet in Hillsboro. The series of interruptions that had begun almost before he had crawled out of bed and continued throughout the morning had left him irritable and impatient. Miss Hawley had been hurriedly dispatched without any definite answer to her query regarding blanket permission for late hours for the girls with permanent baby-sitting employment.

"Why does she think we keep a dean of women around here?" he muttered. "You'd think she could take the responsibilities for her own actions once in a while!"

A timid knock on the door once again rattled the president's concentration.

"Come in," he answered sharply.

Mr. Farley entered and launched forth with effusive apologies for being there on a busy morning.

"What is it you need, Farley?" said Dr. Todd with exasperation.

"It's about the testimony Peter Bradley gave in chapel."

"Well, what was wrong with that?"

"Nothing. I'm just as pleased as anyone that the boy will be

able to stay in school. But I did think as president of the school
you ought to know how it happened."

Dr. Todd pushed his notes aside. "All right, how did it happen?"

"Dr. Herbert made the back payments out of the remainder of
his wife's insurance policy."

Ronald Todd nodded dourly, allowed his chair to revolve a
half turn, and looked out the window. His dad had once said
that God can most use those who don't care who gets the credit.
It seemed necessary for him to relearn this lesson many times.

7

Marty

THE SECOND OF MAY fell on a Tuesday. Marty had jotted the date down on the inside of her notebook cover as a reminder of her roommate's birthday. It really wouldn't have been necessary, however, since Jeanne had dropped a profusion of hints, none too subtly, as soon as they had crawled out of bed that morning. Marty smiled and breathed deeply to savor the freshness of the spring evening. The rains of the two previous months had transformed the Coastal campus and surrounding hillsides into a near-tropical greenery, and the Pacific-Daylig .- Time gift of added twilight hours was more than she could refuse. *For once the studies can wait,* she thought, skipping down the front steps of Harrison Hall.

She strolled down the road toward the main gate, having already informed Pete of her intention to get out and walk for a while. He had promised to eat quickly and be along with the car before her ambition outdid her conditioning. Thus she turned onto the highway feeling carefree and independent. The past six weeks had been so very good. Marty's joy in the Lord and in her Christian friends was unbounded—at times almost too perfect to be real. Since the miraculous settlement of his debts, Pete had relaxed, and she found him more irresistible each day. The only new problem on the horizon was the fact of graduation at the end of the month. Marty had tried not to think about it, but this sort of "ostrich defense" was wearing thin. The day would come. Pete would be going back up to Washington and then on to seminary in New York next fall. For her, summer meant Santa Alberta, a house crowded with Joyce and the children, and friends from a world to which she no longer belonged. The whole prospect was dismal, even when viewed on a warm evening in the verdant countryside.

Her thoughts were interrupted by the blast of a horn from down the road. She turned and waited until the car pulled alongside her.

"You didn't let me get very far," she protested as he reached across the seat to open the door.

"Didn't feel like hanging around the lounge waiting for you to get your exercise. Forgive me this time?"

"Maybe, if you'll get on your knees and beg," she said, climbing in.

"You are a dreamer!" Pete replied as the car again moved forward. "Still want to go into Harwood and get those doughnuts?"

She nodded her response and smiled broadly in his direction. "What's so funny?"

"Nothing," she replied happily. "It's just nice out and I feel good."

"Then come over here a little closer and share all this happiness."

Marty obediently scooted across the seat and rested her head contentedly on his shoulder. "You're a menace to the highway when you drive one-handed," she teased.

"Uh-huh," he agreed, turning and quickly kissing her forehead.

"Listen, buddy, either drive it or park it!"

"I was hoping you'd suggest that," he said, pulling the car off the road onto a sandy strip that fronted an abandoned farm.

"You're impossible tonight!" she laughed.

"Nope, just feeling good, like you are."

"Wouldn't it be nice if we could always feel this good—no

problems or anything," she said dreamily while looking out over the expansive and unkept lawn of the old farm.

"You'd get bored and you know it."

"Maybe, but I'd like to try it for a while."

"What's the matter, little one?" he asked gently. "What's the big problem now?"

"Nothing," she said lightly. "I just don't want anything to change."

Their eyes met for a moment, and then in defensive shyness they both laughed.

"Did I tell you I got a letter from the seminary today?" Pete asked, knowing full well that he hadn't mentioned it.

"So?"

"So they've got a spot reserved for me."

"Great," Marty commented without enthusiasm.

"Why, I thought you'd get all excited," he teased. "Aren't you coming with me?"

"Somehow I don't remember ever having been invited."

"Oh, that. Well, I thought about it, but figured you'd rather stay around Coastal for the next few years and play the field a while."

"Oh, sure. Of course I would."

He stopped smiling and looked at her intently. "You're just eighteen, Marty."

"Uh-huh."

"What do you mean 'uh-huh'? Aren't you going to help me out of this conversation any more than that?"

"No," she said simply.

His hands were laced on top of the steering wheel, and he rested his head upon them for what seemed several minutes to Marty. At last he sat back, his blue eyes deeply serious. "Does it help to know that I'd like to be able to make plans for the future with you? I really wish it were possible, but it isn't. And you know it as well as I do. We have no right to be doing that."

"Is it too much to ask why not?"

"Because God hasn't given any clear indication that He means us for each other."

Marty didn't make any immediate answer. So much was suddenly hanging in the balance. Finally, after brushing some hair away from her eyes, she said, "OK, I'll buy that."

"Well, He hasn't, has He?" Pete insisted.

"Not as far as I know."

"Come on, Marty, I'm not trying to hurt your feelings. But I'm sure God has called me to the mission field, and I know that the wife He has for me is going to be called there too."

"OK, fine. I'm not arguing with you," she said, straightening up and moving back to her side of the car. "In other words, we're supposed to stay good friends for the next couple of weeks, say good-bye at graduation, and then maybe exchange wedding invitations and birth announcements in a few years. OK. Sounds like a winner to me."

"You can be plenty disgusting when you want to be," he muttered.

"Now what did I do?" she asked with feigned innocence. "All I did was agree with everything you said."

"Forget it!" he replied angrily and started the motor. Making a wide U-turn, they headed back for the school. Marty started to remind him about picking up the doughnuts for Jeanne's party, but she wasn't certain she dared try to say anything. The wound that had been opened inside her seemed to be tearing farther apart each minute. She only hoped to make it back to the dorm before the seams burst.

* * *

Kathy McMasters carefully replaced the remaining cookies in their sack. She picked up the wastebasket and began combing the room for leftover cups and napkins.

"You want me to put what's left in these bottles back in Mrs. Dickenson's refrigerator?" asked Jeanne as she finished recapping two bottles of cola.

"Oh, just leave them here. Corrine will finish it off before she goes to bed," Kathy answered. "Jeanne, you don't have to help me clean up. This was your birthday party you know."

"Oh, I don't mind, and everyone else had a stack of things to do."

"What did Marty have to do?" questioned Kathy, still annoyed that Marty hadn't picked up the doughnuts as originally promised. It was just lucky that Mrs. Dickenson had some cookies in her kitchen, and that she had been willing to donate them for the occasion.

"I don't think she's feeling very good tonight. She's been real quiet."

"Maybe we ought to trade roommates for a while. Corrine's been storming around here all week. Hasn't shut up for five seconds."

"What's the matter with her?"

"I really don't know, Jeanne. It kind of worries me sometimes. Corrine makes a lot of noise, but it's hard to tell what she's really thinking. Of course I know she's teed off at me for getting an A on the psych test when she only made a C, and she *did* study a lot longer for it. But that's no reason to take it out on me, is it?"

"No," Jeanne agreed while wiping crumbs off the desk. "If I got mad at Marty every time she beat me in a test, we'd never be on speaking terms."

"It's like Corrine had a chip on her shoulder or something. She's not just mad at me; it's everybody and everything. Might have something to do with school being nearly over. She got this way last year toward the end. I don't think she's looking forward to spending the summer at home."

"Where is she right now?" Jeanne asked, remembering that the room had been vacant for fifteen minutes since the party had broken up.

Kathy frowned. "You won't say anything to anybody, will you?"

"No," was the puzzled reply.

"She's taking a walk; she does it every night."

"But no one's supposed to go out of the dorm after nine o'clock."

"I know, I know."

"But it's dangerous!" Jeanne protested.

Kathy sat down on her rumpled bed. "I know it is, Jeanne. But what am I supposed to do—turn her in to Mrs. Dickenson or Miss Hawley? I've tried talking to her, but she says she gets 'cabin fever' from staying around here all the time. And maybe she does. Corrine's used to living on a ranch."

"She could take her walks in the daytime."

"That's what I told her, but she insists she has to walk at night or she can't sleep."

Jeanne shrugged her broad shoulders hopelessly. "I don't know what to tell you."

"Just pray about it, will you? And don't say anything to anyone, not even Marty. I wouldn't have told you, but I was sure I could trust you to pray with me and not spread the story all over school."

"OK, Kathy," said Jeanne, still troubled. She turned and started for the door. "You want me to empty that basket for you? I have to go down the hall anyway."

"Here," said Kathy, giving the basket a push in Jeanne's direction. "You're not going to be happy until you've done all the dirty work for this party."

"Well, I really appreciate all of you remembering my birthday."

"Go on," directed Kathy. "Oh, yeah, and tell your roommate I think she's a stinker."

"Why?"

"Just tell her. She'll know what I mean."

*   *   *

Marty was deliberately cool toward Pete the next couple of days, and by way of rewarding her behavior he decided to go to a track meet with "the boys" on Friday evening. She accepted his explanation with good humor, knowing she had brought it on herself, and he responded by mentioning the choir concert scheduled the following evening.

After sitting around the dorm on a date night, Marty concluded that there wasn't much sense in sparring with Pete during the last few weeks they would have together. If graduation was going to be the end of everything, well, then there was no need to be miserable any sooner than necessary.

Jeanne spent most of the evening buried in a book, and the dorm was relatively quiet. Shortly before eleven Marty decided to wash her hair and, after hunting down the shampoo and a towel, was ready to leave when someone banged on the door.

"Come on in," she called.

Kathy, concern etched in her face, pushed her way inside. "I've got to talk to you a minute, Jeanne," she said breathlessly.

Marty waited a moment, then sensed she wasn't to be included. "I was just going," she assured Kathy. There was something about Jeanne that prompted confidence from everyone who knew her, and Marty was somewhat accustomed to being left out of these spiritual counseling sessions. It stung a little, but she had to admit that Jeanne had spent much more time getting to know the other girls in the dorm than she had.

As soon as Marty closed the door, Kathy spoke in a heavy whisper, "Corrine's gone!"

"What do you mean?"

"She went out for a walk over two hours ago and hasn't come back."

Jeanne was frightened. "Are you sure she's not around someplace—at the library maybe?"

"It's almost eleven. Everything's closed, and nobody in the dorm has seen her for hours. I even went outside and looked around for a bit. Jeanne, I'm scared!"

The door suddenly opened and Marty reappeared. "Forgot my cream rinse," she apologized.

"Can't we tell Marty?" Jeanne pleaded.

"Oh, I suppose," replied Kathy wearily. "Everybody's going to know before long anyway."

"Corrine's disappeared!" Jeanne announced in hushed tones.

Marty looked at Kathy, awaiting a more graphic explanation.

"She went for a walk a couple of hours ago and hasn't come back."

"You've looked for her, I suppose."

Kathy nodded.

"Well, you'd better tell Mrs. Dickenson."

"Yes, I guess I'll have to, but it's liable to get Corrine in trouble."

"I don't think you have any choice," interjected Jeanne. "Do you want me to go with you?"

"Would you? Maybe you can explain it so it doesn't sound quite so bad."

"I don't know about that," said Jeanne, slipping into her robe and accompanying Kathy out into the hall. "Pray for us, Marty," she called back.

* * *

Marty opened one sleepy eye the next morning and was surprised to observe that Jeanne's bed was empty. Curious as to whether there had been any new developments regarding Corrine's disappearance, she immediately sat up and pulled on her slippers and robe. It was only a little after six, and Marty shuffled groggily out into the hall. Kathy's door was ajar, and she could hear muffled voices inside. After knocking softly, she stuck her head in.

Kathy looked up with a start, then beckoned her to join them. Jeanne was sitting on Corrine's bed, which appeared still untouched.

"Nothing?" Marty questioned.

Kathy shook her head.

"Miss Hawley was just up here to check, but they haven't been able to find any sign of her. The police have been called in, and

Corrine's folks are on their way." Jeanne's serious expression showed traces of the inner excitement which drifted through.

"I suppose there isn't much we can do then."

"Kathy and I have been praying together," Jeanne replied. "I was about ready to come back over to our room and get dressed. Miss Hawley's going to call a meeting down in the lounge in a half hour. She's hoping someone knows something that will help."

"Guess I might as well get dressed too," Marty commented as Jeanne stood up and started for the door.

"Isaiah 40:31," Jeanne said to Kathy, who nodded. "Let's keep trusting."

Marty followed her roommate into the hall, trying unsuccessfully to recall that reference. It was strange that Jeanne who skillfully confused chemical equations never got mixed up on Bible verses. *Maybe that's a special gift,* thought Marty, trying to excuse her own ineptness in this area. The two girls went down the hall to wash and then returned to their room. Neither spoke, although there was no particular need for silence. The dorm was beginning to stir in all corners.

Jeanne methodically slipped into the dress she had worn yesterday, causing Marty to cringe slightly. It was noticeably wrinkled in the back and, even though today was Saturday, she wished that Jeanne might be a little more careful. Of course her roommate was more concerned about Corrine than with what she put on, and Marty sincerely tried to share this genuine concern. It wasn't put on with Jeanne. Marty was interested and even a little worried, but she wasn't able to involve herself to the same extent.

"Have you seen my white shoes?" she asked, breaking the silence.

"No," Jeanne replied. "You didn't leave them over in the shed when we changed for PE yesterday, did you?"

Remembering, Marty nodded her head with disgust. "I wore those old ratty tennis shoes back over here." She tapped her fingers impatiently on the closet door. "Now what am I going to do? I can't wear those red ones with this pink skirt."

Jeanne ignored the problem, walked over to the desk and picked up her Bible.

"Guess I'll have to go down to the storage room and get the straw ones out of my footlocker."

"Is it really all that important?" Jeanne asked with sudden impatience. "I mean, here's Corrine lost, and you're worried about whether your shoes match your skirt."

"I'm not worried about it. But there's enough time for me to find the other pair. Why shouldn't I go look?"

Jeanne gave a shrug of indifference and sat down at the desk, leaving Marty both puzzled and annoyed. Wearing her slippers, she tramped out into the corridor and trudged down the stairs. The lower floor of Cullen was still relatively quiet. Marty crossed the lounge and shuffled past the infirmary to reach the room designated for storage. Limited closet space in the dorm required that the girls leave some of their clothes in trunks and boxes. It was a nuisance, thought Marty with irritation as she opened the door.

An uncurtained small window allowed the early morning dimness to seep in on the dusty collection of luggage, equipment and aging furniture. Marty coughed and switched on the light in order to distinguish her footlocker from the others. She located it in a corner under some boxes and, after unpiling these, dragged it out to the free floor space in the center of the room. Had the shoes been on top she might not have reached for the rickety wooden chair to use in sorting through the contents. In doing so, however, she dislodged a pile of blankets and inadvertently caused the collapse of a makeshift shelter behind the trunks. Marty stepped back in amazement as Corrine's huddled figure was exposed.

"What are you doing down here?"

The husky girl stared at her sullenly. "They were all in here twice last night, and nobody even noticed," she muttered in a low voice.

"You know that everybody's looking for you?" Marty asked incredulously, realizing the answer even as she spoke.

Corrine sighed heavily and leaned back against the wall, showing no interest in further conversation.

"Well, what's the point?" Marty persisted.

Corrine didn't answer. The tears began to course slowly down her cheeks, though her facial expression remained distant and unchanged.

"Is something wrong? Can I help?" asked Marty in softer tones. She was perplexed and now uncertain about this situation. "Corrine?" she said, unable to get the other girl's attention.

"Just go away. You don't care."

"Yes, I do," Marty protested.

Corrine responded with a muffled half laugh, and the tears continued to escape from her red-rimmed eyes. "You couldn't care less, Marty, and you know it. Why should you?" she added bitterly. "You've got everything."

"That's not true."

"Just go away and leave me alone."

"OK," Marty said, putting things back in her locker and closing the top. "But I've got to tell Miss Hawley that you're down here."

"I won't talk to her either."

"That's your privilege, I guess." She began to back toward the door.

"Wait! Don't send Miss Hawley down here," pleaded Corrine, suddenly reversing her attitude. "She'll give me a big lecture, and I don't think I can take that right now."

Marty hesitated in the doorway.

"Is Jeanne upstairs?" Corrine asked.

"Yes."

"Tell her I want to see her. Just Jeanne; don't tell anyone else where I am."

"All right," Marty agreed, doubtful whether she was doing the right thing but anxious to shift the responsibility to someone else. *Maybe Jeanne will know how to handle it,* she thought while hurrying back up to the room.

Several hours later, when the excitement and mystery had subsided, Marty asked Jeanne what had been said that had eventually resulted in both girls going to see Miss Hawley.

"She just told me how she felt about some things. Corrine's really pretty mixed up inside. I think she staged her 'disappearance' just to get some attention. We've all been kind of hard on her in the dorm this year—all our teasing and smart remarks," Jeanne reflected soberly. "Things aren't always what they look like."

"I'm glad you were able to talk to her. She didn't want to tell me anything."

"Oh, I suppose I've been around Corrine more than most of you."

"It's not just Corrine though," Marty continued. "All the girls feel that way about you. Sometimes I'm a little envious."

"Don't be silly," Jeanne protested. "Everybody likes you."

"But they don't trust me or confide in me."

"They don't know you that well."

"You mean I haven't made the effort to really get to know them."

"Well, you're busy, Marty, with studies and with Pete and—"

"Yeah, I'm pretty busy all right," she said ruefully, wondering how many more lessons God had for her to learn this year.

* * *

Among the traditions established during Coastal Bible College's fifteen-year existence was that of an honors chapel held on the last day of classes preceding finals week. On this occasion the senior class sat apart from the rest of the student body, and one of its members brought a farewell message representing the prayers and hopes of the group. Marty had been disappointed when Pete was not chosen to speak, in spite of his repeated claims that he wasn't much of a preacher. He also assured her that he was not in line to receive any of the scholastic cups or other honors to be awarded that morning, but her confidence remained steadfast.

"Why not?"

"For one reason, because my grades haven't been that good. I got C's in freshman English," he told her.

"How could you? You're an English major."

"Just happened, I guess."

"Well, I think you'll at least get that trophy from the Bible department," Marty persisted.

"I couldn't possibly get it. I didn't even turn in a paper, and that's what the award is based on. Give it up, little one. I'm going to get my degree next week. A few months back even that didn't seem likely."

"I don't care. I still think you've earned something special."

"I've got you," he said, grinning, and hand in hand they headed for the mailboxes. The crowd that normally gathered at this spot right before chapel each morning had thinned somewhat when they arrived.

"Get anything?" Marty asked as she dialed the combination to her box.

"Nope, but then I had a card from my folks yesterday."

The little glass door popped open, and she reached inside to withdraw a single letter. "Bet you're kind of excited about seeing them. It's been a long time."

He nodded and looked over her shoulder. "Your mother, huh?"

Marty neatly slit one end of the envelope with a fingernail and quickly scanned the two pages of notepaper. "Are we late?" she asked, still reading as they walked down the hallway.

"A little maybe. What's the news from home?"

"Don't know—haven't found any yet, unless you consider Aunt Edith's broken hip news. Oh, wait, this part's more interesting. Al's been coming over to see Joyce and the kids for the last couple weeks, and he even took Danny to the zoo last Sunday."

"That sounds encouraging."

"I suppose so," Marty replied, refolding the letter and sticking it in her purse . "But even if he decides he wants his family back, won't it just be the same thing all over again? Joyce seems to think he's changed a lot, but he still isn't a Christian and—"

"And you need to give God time to work it out in His way," Pete broke in.

"Oh, I know, I know," she acknowledged as they started downstairs. "I just don't see how Joyce is ever going to be happy married to him. Even if he does get saved, he's still going to be Al."

"Isn't she in love with him?"

"That's what she always says, but I don't see how she really could be."

"Since you don't find him very lovable, you don't see how anyone else could. Right?"

"Right," agreed Marty firmly, knowing he was needling her. "How come you know everything, as usual?" she added with a touch of sarcasm.

He looked a bit sheepish, then gave her hand a squeeze as they parted outside the chapel doors.

Marty slipped into her assigned place just as Dr. Todd stepped briskly to the rostrum. This signaled for automatic quiet throughout the audience. It was not an ordinary chapel gathering; Marty sensed this immediately. Once again she was impressed by the mystique of Coastal. Under normal circumstances a pregraduation affair of this sort, involving the singing of class songs plus testimonies from several students concerning their four years' experience, would have been anything but impressive. Most likely she would have allowed her mind to wander into the area of idle dreams, returning only when the program had concluded. But Coastal was not like Hoover High had been, nor like what State might have been. Or perhaps it was only that she was not like what she had been or might have been. Marty smiled to herself. Whatever the reason, the closely knit bonds of those belonging to Jesus Christ were on display that morning, and the assembled students felt and reacted as a unit.

Pete was the third to give a testimony. For all her wheedling he had not mentioned having any part in the chapel program. *Proud of your humility, aren't you?* Marty thought as he approached the platform, but she edged forward slightly as he started to speak.

"I'd like to share with you the first five verses from the 103rd Psalm: 'Bless the LORD, O my soul: and all that is within me, bless his holy name. Bless the LORD, O my soul, and forget not all his benefits: who forgiveth all thine iniquities; who healeth all thy diseases; who redeemeth thy life from destruction; who crowneth thee with lovingkindness and tender mercies; who satisfieth thy mouth with good things; so that thy youth is renewed like the eagle's.' " Pete closed his Bible and looked out over the audience. "When I came to Coastal, passages like this were familiar to me. For as long as I could remember I had heard them in church as a part of a responsive reading or as the basis for some lesson. But though I would have defended the truth of those verses because they were a part of God's Word, they really brought forth little personal response on my part. And it is in this area that God has so greatly worked in my life since that time four years ago. He has taught me to study the Word for myself and to apply it, not generally but specifically to my own life. With the help of many of the faculty and also many of my fellow students, God has become very real and a very active force in my everyday experience. And I praise Him for it, knowing that without this, I cannot hope to serve Him acceptably in the future."

Annette Perkins was next to speak and, by the time she had finished, the film had cleared from Marty's eyes sufficiently for her to look up from the floor. Dr. Todd stepped forward again and without further delay announced the award recipients. Quiet

Sandra Reed and a smiling Hal Frazier accepted the plaques for the highest overall scholastic average. And Hal, now beaming, was called back to receive official notification of a scholarship grant for graduate study at a university next year. There were several others: Tom Hailey taking the honors in the Bible department competition, Susan Howard holding the Christian service trophy, and finally two members of the junior class receiving tuition scholarships for the following year.

"This concludes the regular yearly awards," Dr. Todd said. "But we do have one additional honor to present. To my knowledge this marks the first time that a freshman has had a part in honors chapel but, in view of the fact that this $100 award comes from a national competition, I believe it only fitting that it be presented at this time. The faculty is extremely proud to announce that third place in the Literary Journal's fiction contest has been given to Miss Jeanne Robbins of Coastal Bible College."

There were several audible gasps of surprise at this announcement. Then Marty watched proudly as Jeanne made her way to the platform and with shaking hand accepted the check and accompanying certificate. It was a moment of triumph, and Marty noted with astonishment that she was as elated as if the moment had been her own. Her heart was full for Jeanne and for Pete and Tom, Sandra, Hal and all the others, but most of all for the Saviour who had made her a part of this group and a part of Himself.

*   *   *

The activities of the final week of school blurred in Marty's mind as they swept by. So much happened simultaneously, or at least consecutively, and this coupled with late-hour cram sessions left nerves frayed and emotions easily stirred. Stoical Jeanne had melted into tears twice on the night preceding the humanities final, but had limped through the exam with better than usual success. In fact, there was some indication that Miss

Robbins might eventually blossom into a respectable scholar, and she gratefully credited Marty with the improvement.

"Really, Marty, I think just living with you has helped me a lot in my studies. I never was around anyone who was so organized before and, you know, it does make a difference!"

Laughing, Marty put her arm around her roommate's shoulder. "Well, I'm glad that I contributed something to the team of Robbins and Miller this year."

"Don't be silly; you've contributed a lot."

"Nowhere near what I've gained though."

The two girls were walking back to the dorm following the Thursday noon meal. They were tired, and the warm spring sunshine seemed more conducive to a nap than to further study.

"Have you made your mind up about coming back next year?" Jeanne asked.

"There's never been any question, at least not since the first couple of months of school."

"Well, I didn't know for sure if you and Pete—" Jeanne faltered.

"What did I say to make you think that Pete and I had any plans for next year?"

"Nothing. I just thought maybe—"

"I'm going to be back at Coastal, as long as the Lord makes it possible. Pete's going to seminary in New York. He's already been accepted."

They went up the front steps of Cullen but, instead of going inside, Jeanne walked over to the old hammock and flopped down. "New York's a long ways away," she said.

"Yes, I've thought of that more than a few times this week."

"Are you in love with him?"

Marty sat down, and the swing made a protesting creak. "What do all your books say? How are you supposed to know whether you're in love or not?"

Jeanne paused and considered the question. "I don't know. Don't you just 'feel' it or something?"

"I'm asking you."

"Well, I once read a story where the heroine thought she couldn't live without this fellow, and that's when she was sure it was love."

"It would hardly be right for a Christian to make any person other than the Lord that important in her life, would it?"

"No," Jeanne agreed. "Oh, I'm sorry. I never should have asked something like that."

"It's OK. I guess the problem is that I don't really know the answer. Or else I'm not ready to admit it even to myself yet. Come on, I want to lie down for a while before starting in on the books again." Marty got to her feet.

"Do you have time to go over the study questions with me?"

"We'll find time."

The lazy afternoon drifted on into evening, and a quiet and meditative mood settled over the campus. Occasionally it was punctured by hysterical waves of laughter, when one of the school's habitual pranksters seized the opportunity for releasing built-up tensions. For the most part, however, life remained quite serious until the conclusion of the last exam on Friday morning, after which a full-scale celebration broke loose. Into this suddenly relaxed atmosphere moved the confusion of packing and the inevitably difficult good-byes for those who were not waiting over for graduation services the next day.

Jeanne said she considered herself a VIP to have Pete and Marty take her to the station that afternoon, and the three of them stood eyeing the clock as they waited for her bus to pull in. It arrived on schedule.

"Well, have a good time at the banquet tonight," she said, picking up her overnight case.

"OK." Marty smiled. "I'll write you all about it."

"So will I," Pete added, "only I'll tell you what really happened!"

"Bye. See you in September."

"In September," Marty echoed, and she leaned back against

Pete as they watched the familiar stocky figure disappear into the interior of the large cross-country vehicle. Jeanne found a seat by an older woman and managed to peer over her companion's head in order to wave a few more times.

Marty was aware of how very much she would miss Jeanne over the next few months but, as they had said, "in September." It was infinitely more difficult to contemplate saying good-bye to Pete, without any assurance that their relationship could ever be resumed. *The Lord giveth, and the Lord taketh away,* she thought, feeling that this was perhaps not exactly what Job had in mind when he said it, but the sentiment was appropriate, though not terribly comforting. These thoughts plagued her that afternoon while she completed as far as possible the task of packing her things. Her folks would arrive in time for commencement tomorrow, and in another twenty-four hours it would be all over. She'd be Marty Miller—Joe Miller's girl, Joyce Miller's sister, part of Santa Alberta, California, a native no less. It seemed far away and rather frightening.

The spring banquet honoring the graduates was held annually in Harwood's largest hotel. It was a less tightly knit school event than the other formal affairs of the year. Alumni were present, as were relatives and close friends of some of the students. Marty's initial shyness over sharing this evening with Pete's parents and his brother, Craig, had melted in a matter of minutes. They were warm individuals, lacking perhaps in some of the goods and experiences of her own background, but lacking nothing as human beings. She now had some insight as to what had molded Pete, and she was grateful to this couple, though she had no way of expressing it. The meal and entertainment lasted until 10:30 P.M., and the "entertainment" had included, as was traditional, the announcement of several engagements. Marty found herself blushing uncontrollably and hoped that none of the Bradley clan had noticed this.

The banquet finally concluded, the five of them drove down to Hillsboro where the senior Bradleys and Craig were to spend the night with friends. The parents excused themselves with brief good-nights and slipped into the house. Craig lingered, suggesting that all would-be preachers needed a chaperone when they dated good-looking girls. He might have continued if his dad hadn't called back from the doorway in a tone that left no room for uncertainty.

"Don't do anything I wouldn't do," he said, reluctantly getting out.

"That gives me a lot of working space," grinned Pete, turning the key in the ignition. He backed the car out into the street, shifted, and pulled away from his still-watching younger brother.

"Where are we going?" Marty asked.

"You hungry?"

"Not hardly!"

"Well, there's a little lake between here and Harwood. I thought we might drive down there and talk for a while."

"Talk?" she said, teasing.

"You had something else in mind?"

"Not me, I like to talk."

"What'd you think of my family?" he asked, changing the subject.

"I liked them—very much."

"That's good. I do too. Did you hear Mom say that Craig's thinking about applying at Coastal for next year?"

"Really? I thought he wasn't too much sold on the idea of Bible school."

"He hasn't been up to now, but this last year has settled him down quite a bit."

They turned onto a side road and traveled about two miles before reaching a sign pointing toward Portor Lake.

"Where'd you find out about this place?" Marty questioned as he eased the car over rut-pocked dirt road.

"You forget I've lived around this area for four years."

"I haven't forgotten. I'm just beginning to wonder how you

spent those first three! That probably explains your C's in fresh-man English."

"Well, not entirely. No, I came here fishing one Easter vacation when I stayed on campus, but I haven't been back since. For all I know, the lake may have dried up."

As they rounded a bend in the road, the view which stretched before them revealed that the lake had not dried up. Instead, it was an isolated spot of beauty, shadowed and enveloped by trees and dotted with small wooden docks. Attached to these were rowboats, indistinguishable by color in the moonlight and weaving only slightly on the glimmering surface of the water.

"Like it?" he asked, quietly bringing the car to a stop in front of one of these collections of pilings and fishing boats.

"It's beautiful," she replied simply.

"I don't think anyone's apt to bother us out here."

Marty laughed, "If I didn't know you better, I think I'd start getting scared!"

"I really did bring you out here to talk," he said seriously. "There's so much that needs to be said. And there've been several times in the last couple of weeks that I've tried to get started, and then just couldn't. I haven't really been sure of what I ought to say."

She shifted uncomfortably, then took his hand and tenderly ran her finger over the back of it. "Pete, don't feel you have to explain anything. I understand. I really do. I knew what you meant when we talked about it before, but I guess I was just out of sorts that night. It's OK with me, really it is. We're both young and have a lot of years ahead. And by next fall when we won't be seeing each other all the time, whatever we feel or don't feel won't seem so important. I'm very thankful to the Lord for giving us this friendship. You've meant so much in my Christian life, and I'll never forget a moment of this year."

"Are you about through?" he asked when she paused.

"Well, I guess so."

"Then may I finish what I started to say?"

"Of course," she replied meekly.

"I love you, Marty."

Tears formed in her eyes, and the words that should have come, stuck in her throat. "Oh, Pete," she cried softly and threw her arms around his neck. He held her tightly.

"Is this supposed to tell me how you feel?" he asked, brushing her dampened cheeks with his lips.

· "I love you, Pete," she whispered.

"This doesn't solve any of our problems, Marty. You know that."

"Uh-huh," she replied, reaching for her purse and a much needed piece of tissue.

"It makes everything more complicated."

"Uh-huh."

He smiled, and he helped her wipe the tears. "I've prayed about this a lot. It seemed that if God had intended me to fall in love with you, He would have worked out all the other details too, like your being called to the mission field, and the two of us being so far apart next year and all the rest. But the last couple of days it has seemed so clear that our love is something He has given and that we should accept it without tying on any conditions. When He opens the next door, that's the time to take the next step. But until then I want to, and I'm going to, love you, and I don't care if you know it or if anyone else knows it."

"And if God never opens any more doors for us?"

"Then we will still have had something beautiful. And as long as we never abuse the beauty of it, then there can be nothing but good memories no matter what sort of separate ways our lives may take."

"You're wonderful."

"You're the wonderful one. A lot of girls wouldn't think that was much of a declaration of affection. And I'm not really promising or guaranteeing a thing—just telling you how much

I want to give it a try, and not shutting out the possibility that God may take care of the details for us."

"I want it that way too, Pete. Somehow I'd been thinking that it had to be all or nothing. And since it obviously couldn't be 'all,' well—it just didn't leave very much."

He gazed out the window as a sudden breeze stirred the water, causing the little boats to bob and pull on their lines. "It won't be easy, Marty. Writing letters will get kind of boring after a while, and you know I haven't got the money to come down to see you this summer."

She nodded, though a dim future seemed far removed at the moment.

"Then next year at school, you're not going to find it much fun sitting around the dorm every weekend while everyone else is out having a big time. Maybe if I wasn't so selfish I could tell you to go ahead and date anyway, but just thinking about it tears me up completely."

"I don't want to go out with anyone else."

"Not now, but what about six months from now?"

"I thought these were the little details we were going to let God handle."

Pete grinned and nodded. "You're right. See how good you are for me! You're always bringing me up short just when I need it."

"Maybe this next year with all those long, quiet weekends will give me a chance to really search out God's will regarding the mission field. I've been praying about it already, but it's so hard to tell whether it's God speaking to me or just my feelings for you that make me lean in that direction."

"I think you'll have to come to the point that you're sure God wants you to go and that you're willing, even if it means going alone."

"That may take some time."

"I can wait, little one. Believe me, I'll be waiting."